CW01496695

A Jubilee

Murder

A Three Villages Cosy Mystery

Book One

JP Fraser

A Three Villages Mystery

A Jubilee Murder

A Jubilee Murder

A Three Villages Cosy Mystery

Book One

Copyright © 2022 by JP Fraser

ISBN: 9798486089343

Cover design by JP Fraser.

Website: www.jpfraserbooks.weebly.com

A Three Villages Mystery

One

Kent
The Garden of England
June 1977

rs Popplewell was difficult to miss at the best of times, being grim of face, stout of build and big of gob. She was perennially garbed in some kind of semi-rigid tweed ensemble, with wispy grey hair that peeked out from beneath what looked like a squashed trilby hat. She waved at me energetically, flinging her arms around like washing clinging to a line on a breezy day.

I groaned as I glanced in the rearview mirror. No, there was no one else in sight on the empty tree-lined lane. Mrs Popplewell was flagging me down and I was going to have to stop. Eye contact had been made and she knew she had me in her clutches. I brought Ernie to a halt by the side of the road, his little eleven hundred engine chugging away contentedly.

A Three Villages Mystery

'Hello Mrs Popplewell,' I shouted as I struggled to wind the window down, sweaty fingers slipping on the handle. 'Lovely morning.'

'Catriona, my dear, have you heard?' she demanded, looking ready to explode.

'Heard what?'

She rolled her eyes, making no attempt to disguise her irritation. The truth was, of course, that she relished being the bearer of bad news. The worse the news, the more she enjoyed it. 'He's struck again. The Pemble house this time, on Pond Lane.' Noting my blank look of confusion, which resembled that of a chimpanzee given a slide rule and asked to perform advanced calculus, she clarified her statement. 'All over the front of the house, it was. All over. It'll take some scrubbing to get that out, I can tell you.'

This was not a great deal of help, but after a few seconds, something began to click in the back of my head as a dimly remembered report began to surface. "Struck again" and "all over the front of the house" latched onto the thought.

'Ah,' I said slowly, in a noncommittal tone, just in case my mind was leading me down the wrong path completely. 'You mean the baked bean bandit?'

She frowned at me, glaring with annoyance. Whether this was because of my evident dim-wittedness, or the Aberdeen accent that she seemed to find so grating, I couldn't tell. 'I am not sure it is appropriate to assign such flippant monikers to such a crime, dear. This reign of terror is a serious and potentially disastrous business for the village.' She sniffed the air, her nose screwing up.

There was a faint whiff of manure about. It mixed with the honeysuckle on the other side of the wall and they formed a sickly cocktail. On one side of the road were open fields that stretched halfway to Maidstone, while on the other was dense woodland, beech and white poplar overhanging the lane.

'Of course not,' I agreed, suitably chastised and wanting nothing more than to escape. 'Have the police been called this time?'

She snorted. 'They have, for all the good that would do. Too busy harassing innocent people to care about the real criminals.'

I saw the scowl deepen and wondered if my existence was further darkening her mood, but then I heard the sound of another car approaching from behind. I glanced in the mirror and saw a flash of scarlet and chrome, recognising the silhouette instantly. There was only one person in the village who had a car like that. It was a little… Now what was it called? Oh, yes. Triumph Spitfire. Probably a little flashy for my taste, unlike my own trusty Ernie the Escort. Ernie had character, if nothing else. He also had bright orange front wings and a red drivers' door, none of which in any way matched the rest of the pale blue bodywork. Character? Yes. Style? Not so much.

'Here she comes,' Mrs Popplewell grumbled. 'Lady muck herself.'

A Three Villages Mystery

Veronica Castle really was no lady in any way other than the strict biological sense, and it seemed that since arriving in the village two years previously, she had done little to endear herself to the locals. I was hardly one to talk, being an in-aboot comer myself, but unlike Veronica I had not gone out of my way to antagonise anyone and everyone I came into contact with.

The car came to an abrupt stop just behind Ernie, and the crunching of loose gravel over the tarmac was accompanied by the coarse shriek of a horn being abused.

'Sorry, Mrs Popplewell,' I said. 'I'd best be getting out of the way.'

'You just stay right where you are, dear,' she ordered, actually pointing an accusing finger at me. 'Her ladyship can wait for once in her privileged life.' It was worth noting that the Popplewells could trace their lineage back to Tudor times, and she had inherited the family estate some years earlier. So she was not exactly a stranger to privilege herself.

There was another blast on the horn, this time almost making a tune: biiiib, bib-bib-bib, biiiib!

'I'll just move a little closer into the side,' I shouted, earning myself another glare, but I edged Ernie closer to the pavement until the tyres squeaked against the kerb. There was the revving of an engine and the Spitfire edged past, Veronica careful not to scratch the paintwork on the little sports car. I had the feeling she wasn't quite as bothered about Ernie. Admittedly, he did look something of a mess, but to me that just added to his charm.

A Jubilee Murder

The Spitfire roared away as soon as it was clear and disappeared round the corner toward Ashfield Lane, but Veronica had ensured she gave me a look of cold disdain as she went past.

'Honestly,' Mrs Popplewell said, tutting like a disappointed school mistress, 'everyone is in such a hurry these days.

'Oh I know,' I agreed, looking down at the clock on the dashboard that I knew was an hour slow, but that I hadn't gotten around to putting right when the clocks had gone forward a few weeks earlier.

'Tell me, dear, what plans do you have for the jubilee? I trust you will be contributing in some way? I do hope so. It's terribly important for newcomers to the community to lend their support to important local events, don't you agree?'

'Absolutely,' I replied, and quickly tried to think of something I could do. I'd heard about the jubilee celebrations, of course. As the day approached, the television and papers seemed unable to focus on anything else, but I had hoped to largely avoid the festivities. Now I realised I would have to come up with something, and quick. My hesitation was clearly telling, and before I could come up with my own low-key suggestion, Mrs Popplewell leapt in with the inevitable "suggestion", and my fate was sealed.

'I would have thought that you would be entering the baking contest, my dear. They are looking for entrants for Her Majesty's favourite cake; did you know?'

A Three Villages Mystery

Oh I knew all right. I'd been hearing mutterings about this particular event for weeks, and had studiously avoided being cajoled, bullied or browbeaten into taking part. There had recently been a piece in one of the tabloids, alleging that the Queen had a particular fondness for chocolate cake. Okay, who doesn't? But apparently not a day would go by without her indulging in a slice of chocolate biscuit cake. I didn't place a great deal of stock in the veracity of these reports, but the Downscliffe Jubilee Committee had taken this on board and pursued the idea with gusto. Now, the esteemed judge would be sampling upwards of a dozen chocolate biscuit cakes "in Her Majesty's honour". I'm sure Her Maj would be thrilled to learn this. And who would be the one to pass judgement over the entries? None other than Downscliffe's resident food celebrity: Veronica Castle. *The* Veronica Castle, star of her very own cookery programme on Southern Television. The last thing I wanted was to have my culinary efforts adjudicated by Lady Muck, but there seemed to be no getting out of it now. I had been well and truly cornered by an expert. Not to mention cajoled, bullied and browbeaten into submission.

'Well my son Fergus will be in the fancy dress competition, obviously, and I was thinking of entering the baking contest,' I blethered, seeing all hope abandon me.

'Oh, that's wonderful,' my assassin beamed, and there seemed to be an almost maniacal glee in her remark.

I was sure that nothing would have given her greater pleasure than to see the new girl get torn to shreds by

A Jubilee Murder

Veronica Castle. The celebrity had previously written a quite scathing review in the Mercury of my bread pudding, which I sold to one of the local pubs, The Old Badger. Apparently, even though it seemed to be popular with the pub's patrons, according to her it was "a stodgy mess of confectionery excess, like a Lucozade drizzle cake that floated limply in a lake of insipid custard". So it was safe to say that she was not a fan, and I had no great desire to be publicly sacrificed at the jubilee.

I had also just condemned Fergus, my ten-year-old boy, to his own ritual humiliation at the fancy dress contest. We had briefly discussed this, but he had been adamant that he wanted to go as a Dalek, and there was no way – absolutely no way – that he might consider anything else. I quietly let the subject drop after that, and hoped that he would not remember until it was far too late. Now it looked as though I would have to say goodbye to my trusty sink plunger. It would be needed in Fergus's campaign to rule the galaxy.

'Well, I must be getting on,' I said, hearing the note of fatalistic resignation in my voice.

'Of course, dear. I expect you will be needing to practice your cake making skills. And do make sure you tie your hair back, won't you dear? This is a chocolate cake, not a chocolate and ginger concoction.'

She pursed her lips, clearly finding herself most amusing. I didn't, but politely chuckled along nonetheless. On occasion, I would try to describe myself as a fiery redhead, like a Scottish Rula Lenska, only without the charm, talent or stunning looks of the Rock Follies actress. There was no getting away from it; I was, undeniably, ginger, with matching freckles that made me look as though a tin of tomato soup had just exploded in my face.

'You don't want another incident like your bread pudding debacle,' she continued, twisting the knife just a little bit more.

It wasn't generally in my nature to use extreme violence against defenceless old women, but I was rapidly coming to the realisation that this wasn't a completely inviolable rule. I just allowed myself a brief moment of rapture as I allowed the images to play out in my mind: Mrs Popplewell with a broken nose; Mrs Popplewell lying on the pavement with a cracked jaw; Mrs Popplewell accidentally and repeatedly run over. Ah, that felt good, but now it was time to return to reality. I wanted to come up with a response slightly more erudite than "oh shut up, you pompous old bag", but I was not that quick at inventing ingenious ripostes. Instead, I just smiled as sweetly as I could manage, flicked a lock of unruly ginger hair away from my face, and pulled away slowly, waving in as friendly a manner as I could muster.

There was a crunch of gravel and the squeak of hubcap on the kerb, and a few seconds later I had rounded the corner and lost sight of Mrs Popplewell. I could finally relax a bit. My sighs of relief are not generally terribly ladylike, and I would usually end up blowing an expressive, if thoroughly undignified, raspberry. Today, I sounded more like a balloon deflating. Talk about every man's dream.

Ahead was the turning onto Ashfield Lane, where my sweet little bungalow sat. To the left was the cricket pitch, and beyond that the local church. There was no cricket today, what with it being a Friday, and the pavilion was closed. They called it a pavilion, but that was overstating it, just a tad. It was nothing more than a wooden shack with a sagging roof and timbers that hadn't seen a lick of paint in thirty years or more.

St Luke's Church was far more impressive, with an elegant nave and imposing tower. The village had celebrated its eight hundredth anniversary the year before – the same year that the United States had celebrated two hundred years of independence.

What caught my eye today was not the arcane stonework, golden weathervane glinting in the sunshine or the intricate stained glass, but the small scarlet sports car that was parked outside. I had never heard that Veronica expressed much interest in the church, so it seemed odd for her to be parked there. Did she have some relative buried in the graveyard? Possibly, although I was sure that she too was a more recent arrival to the village with no prior connections to the area.

I shrugged it off. There were too many people in this village with their noses in everybody else's business, and I did not want to become one of them. Determined that I wasn't ready to go completely native, I turned onto Ashfield Lane and dropped a gear. Ernie didn't like hills at the best of times.

I now had other things to worry about, and Veronica Castle's newfound interest in the church quickly sank into the dark recesses of my mind.

I had a cake to work on, and a Dalek to make.

Two

I struggled with the key in the front door. It had recently started to stick, and there was a knack to pulling the key out just enough for it to catch and turn. At some point, I would have to get it fixed, hopefully before I got locked out of my own house. This was one of the many, many things that needed to be fixed in our little bungalow. There was also a faint whiff of unburned petrol in the air from Ernie, who sat in the driveway cooling off. He was clearly finding the drive up the hill increasingly tiring, bless him.

Eventually, after a good fifteen seconds of cursing and struggling, I fell into the doorway and slipped on the mail that lay on the doormat. I had a quick flick through, checking to see if there was anything important. There was a letter from the water board, no doubt telling me that their rates were going up. How wonderful. On a happier note, there was a post card from my friend Becky. She was one of the few people from Aberdeen with whom I had stayed in contact, and was on holiday in Majorca. The card showed half a dozen pools in various luxury resorts that I was pretty sure would not be quite as grand and opulent as they tried to make out. Still, Becky seemed to be having a great time and none of the kids seemed to have drowned, fallen off cliffs or been electrocuted, so that was a plus. There was also a letter from my agent. Sales of my first cookbook were bobbing away nicely. Not enough to give Fanny Craddock any nightmares, but not bad. The second book was actually doing quite well; better than expected, and the publisher was "eagerly awaiting" an update on the third cookbook's progress. So was I. I still had no clear idea what the theme would be, but trusted that it would all work out in the end.

As long as I didn't get any more bile-infused reviews from Veronica Castle, I should be okay.

I have to admit, I was still annoyed with Mrs Popplewell, but probably more annoyed with myself, if I'm going to be honest. I'd allowed her to get under my skin and goad me into action, and now I was stuck with two jobs that I could really have done without. Not only that, but I was opening myself up to more career threatening grief from dearest Veronica.

I dropped the pile of letters onto the coffee table in the living room and went for a filch about in the pantry. If I was going to make a chocolate biscuit cake, I at least needed to make sure I had the ingredients which, naturally, I didn't. This was rapidly turning into one of those days. As I checked through shelves piled high with jars of mixed spice, dried fruit peel, packets of sultanas, tubs of baking powder and almonds – everything that a well-stocked larder should have – I wondered how I would make a Dalek for a ten-year-old. I'd already become resigned to the fact that my sink plunger would be redesignated as a… Actually, what *was* the sink plunger on a Dalek for? Then I would need about fifty-odd balls to stick on the sides and a pudding basin for the head. I rubbed my eyes as I realised what a job this would be. There might need to be some renegotiation with Fergus. Suddenly, making a prize-winning cake did not seem quite so daunting.

The next couple of hours were spent flicking through my cookbooks, which were packed with scraps of paper used as rudimentary bookmarks when I found promising recipes.

The basic idea of a chocolate biscuit cake couldn't be simpler: butter, sugar, eggs, biscuits and chocolate. Easy-peasy. Couldn't be simpler, but I had to get this right. Maybe a touch of golden syrup to soften it a smidge? How about a squeeze of lemon juice? Or a dash of allspice? There were a million and one different things I could try, just to make my cake stand out from the rest, but I could never be sure in advance what that secret ingredient might be. All I knew was that it had to be good, and not give Veronica any excuse to complain. I'd give her "a stodgy mess of confectionery excess". As much as I'd tried to put it behind me and move on, that review in the Mercury still rankled.

After a couple of hours of scouring cookery books

and making notes, I had a good idea of what I would be trying first. I just needed a couple of things from the shops in order to start experimenting.

A jarring ding-dong from the doorbell put paid to any more theoretical recipe making, and I did a thirty-second frenzied tidy up, piling cookbooks onto the coffee table, scraps of paper poking out at all angles.

I stood up straight and roughly smoothed down the creases in my dungarees, and straightened the t-shirt beneath. The Aladdin Sane one, with David Bowie's face and the lightning flash. I swore I would probably die in that t-shirt. It even came with its own ventilation, the stitching in one shoulder having come away. I wrestled with the front door latch for several seconds – it was no easier to open from the inside – and found a very flustered Debbie Dugdale waiting on the doorstep.

'Hey sunshine. You will not believe what's happened,' she spluttered, leaning against the doorframe. I assumed she had just run up the road from her house.

'I don't know; try me.'

Debbie shook her head, taking a few seconds to catch her breath, dark brown, almost black hair hanging like limp curtains over her face. She lived about six doors down the road from Frisky Pigeons. That was the name of my little bungalow, by the way. In an area like this, most houses did not have numbers. When I bought the place the year before, "Downs View" had seemed such a boring, prosaic appellation, and I hated it immediately. I loved the house as soon as I saw it, but the name just *had* to go.

A Jubilee Murder

Frisky Pigeons was much more me, even if some of the locals did raise a disapproving eyebrow or two when they heard it.

Debbie's house was a much more reserved, "The Willows", which the local landed gentry found much more agreeable. However, Debbie herself could not, by any stretch of the imagination, be described in such a way. She was brash, vulgar, loud and uncouth. She could belch like a trucker, and some of her burps would rattle the glass in the window frames.

I liked Debbie immensely.

Like me, she was an in-aboot comer, although she was not from quite as far afield as Aberdeen. She was an immigrant from South London. Or "Saff London", as she would put it. She was a couple of years younger than me, and was still mourning the arrival of the dreaded thirty milestone and the passing of her youth, which she could just see disappearing over the horizon. She and her husband, Tony, had moved to the village a couple of years earlier, escaping the squalor and violence of Peckham. They had twins – not identical – and did not want them growing up among the skinheads and junkies who had taken over the capital in recent years.

'Mrs Popplewell told me about it earlier,' I said, hoping to take the wind out of Debbie's sails.

'You heard already?'

'Aye. The Pembles' house on Pond Lane, wasn't it?'

'Eh? Pembles?'

I began to realise that the wind may soon be

returning to her sails. 'You mean the bean fiend, don't you? The notorious Downscliffe baked bean bandit? Scourge of front doors and windows throughout the land?'

'He's hit the Pembles' house? Blimey. No, that's news to me, but it's not what I'm talking about. I meant did you see the ambulance and rozzers go up the road?'

'No?' Now this did sound exciting. I don't think I was a gossip in Mrs Popplewell's league, but I wouldn't pass up on something that sounded as juicy as this. 'Tell you what; come in and have a drink. This sounds too good for the doorstep.'

Debbie's eyes lit up at the sound of the word "drink", and followed me through to the kitchen, after she had slammed the door three times to get the latch to secure.

'What'll it be?' I asked. 'Wine or fruity juice?'

'What do you think?'

'Wine it is, then.' I opened the cupboard under the sink, the door squeaking like a mouse had just been caught in the hinges, and withdrew a bottle of potato wine. I'd knocked up a five-gallon batch while I was still in Aberdeen, and had brought it with me when I moved. Plonking a pair of brown-smoked glasses on the pine table, I poured a generous measure of wine and slid it across to Debbie. After nine months of lying undisturbed, the cloudiness of the tattie wine had all but disappeared, and the liquid now resembled a crisp, pale apple juice. For myself, I took a half-empty bottle of Shloer from the fridge and filled the other glass, before prizing open the lid of an old Quality Street tin, half full with party rings, custard creams and bourbon biscuits. I'd already polished off the pink wafers.

'Okay, spill it, sister,' I said, and watched as Debbie took a tentative sip. It wasn't quite paint thinner, although it certainly made my eyes water whenever I tried it. It was potent stuff, and would also give me a curious tingling at the very top of my head and make the backs of my eyeballs sting. I waited for a reaction, for the coughing and spluttering that normally accompanied a taste of my homemade wine, but Debbie was made of sterner stuff than that. Lord knows what she must have grown up on. Probably creosote cocktails, I would have wagered.

'Well,' Debbie said, leaning forward as if imparting some forbidden knowledge, 'you'll never guess what's happened.'

'We've already been through this. Just tell me.'

She grinned and took another swig. 'You know your friend Veronica Castle?'

'Oh good grief, what has she done this time?' It was only then that I recalled Debbie mentioning an ambulance and "rozzers", as she had so eloquently referred to the local constabulary.

'Only gone and killed herself,' Debbie said with a hint of triumph in her voice.'

'No!' I sat there, glass of fruity and decidedly non-alcoholic wine halfway to my lips, but mouth wide open in shock. It had only been a couple of hours since I had seen Veronica, looking glamorous as always, and just as disagreeable as ever.

'Straight up. The way I hear it, old Wally Moore was walking past her house and saw the front door wide open. He went to investigate – you know what a nosy old so-and-so he is – and that's when he found her, hanging in the hallway right by the door.'

'Hanged? Seriously? Wow. That's horrible.' I couldn't believe it. Veronica Castle? Committing suicide? I just couldn't envisage someone like that killing herself. She was just too arrogant and in love with herself to take her own life. At least, that was the impression she gave. Maybe I had her all wrong, but somehow, I doubted it. 'I only saw her this morning,' I said absently as my mind raced. 'On Church Lane. I'd been ambushed by Mrs Popplewell.'

'Ooh, nasty. Need any help getting the two-dozen knives out of your back?'

'Naw, I had my bulletproof vest on. Veronica drove past. Nearly took my wing mirror off as she did so.'

'Then you and Mrs Pimply-whatsit could've been the last people to see her before… you know.' She made a throat slashing motion with her hand, accompanied by a theatrical grimace.

'No, I don't think we were the last ones. A couple of minutes later, I saw her car parked outside the church. I thought that was a wee bit odd as she was to religion what Joseph Stalin was to the free market economy.'

'Maybe she was saying a last little prayer before she did it?'

A Jubilee Murder

I shrugged. 'Maybe. Just seems a bit odd, though. I mean she was hardly the religious type.'

'People do odd things when they're about to kill themselves. I mean, suicide *is* a bit odd in itself, innit? Not beyond the realms of possibility for her to act out of character before she did it.'

'*If* she did it,' I added.

'Well it sounds like she was pretty dead to me.'

'No, I mean, suppose *she* didn't do it.'

Perhaps I hadn't chosen the best moment to throw in that possibility, as Debbie was in mid-swig of a generous gulp of tattie wine. She didn't quite spit it across the kitchen, but some definitely went the wrong way and she spluttered, sneezing when some of the sweet fire liquid went up her nose.

'You mean you think she was murdered?' she demanded, once it was clear there wouldn't be a second death on Ashfield Lane today.

'No, no, no. Well maybe. It's possible, don't you think? I mean, Veronica was a lot of things, but I never had her down as clinically depressed. Certainly not depressed enough to commit suicide.'

'You're right,' Debbie agreed, wiping her chin with her sleeve. 'I'm sure lots of people would have a motive.'

'Aye, me for a start.'

'And me,' she said with a chuckle. 'Generally speaking, if there's any bitching and mithering to be done around here, I like it to be coming from me. This slides down a treat, by the way,' Debbie said, waving her glass

23

in front of my face, just a dribble of wine sloshing around in the bottom.

'Need a top up?'

'Oh, since you're offering, don't mind if I do.'

I poured another generous splash of wine for her.

'You not having one?' she asked, seeming to only just notice that I wasn't joining her.

'Nope. I'm driving this afternoon. It's my turn to pick up the kids.'

'Oh, so it is.' Debbie knew full well that it was my turn, and her smug look confirmed it. 'I'd better have another one for you, then, seeing as you're being Miss Goody Two-Shoes.'

'If you have any more, I'll have to carry you home, and I'm not doing that without a block-and-tackle and a wheelbarrow.' A thought suddenly popped into my head, and it must have shown on my face. I've never been very good at hiding these things, and Debbie was excellent at reading me.

'What? You've had an idea, haven't you? I know your scheming face, and it looks just like that.'

'This isn't my scheming face,' I protested.

'Oh stroll on, that is completely your scheming face.'

'It's still not, but I was wondering, how would you feel about taking a wander up there?'

'What, to Veronica's house?'

'Aye.'

'It'll be crawling with the gendarmes right now. But

I guess there'd be no harm in just sauntering past, I suppose.'

'Good,' I said, standing and putting my almost empty glass on the draining board. 'Get a move on and drink up,' I said, grabbing my handbag and sunglasses from the kitchen table. The handbag was an optional extra that was more akin to a comfort blanket. The sunglasses were an absolute necessity.

'Now? But I need to pee,' Debbie complained with almost a note of panic.

'Well you know where the cludgie is; go and pee! But I want to get there before the rozz— Before the police leave.'

Three

shfield Lane was a good half a mile from the centre of the village, and being so far removed, it was almost a community in its own right. Forty houses, no two being remotely similar, lined one side of the narrow lane. On the other was open fields that stretched down to the church, only the tower of which being visible from this vantage point. The field was covered in a lush carpet of green, the wheat crop faring better this year than the furnace-like hell of the previous summer.

Veronica Castle's house was a little more than a dozen doors up from Frisky Pigeons, a grand, palatial building with sharply slanted roofs – roofs in the plural, as this structure was clearly designed by a stoner in the sixties. My little bungalow was much older, having been built sometime in the twenties or thirties. The deeds to the property were unclear, and nine months earlier, I had been more interested in getting a place quickly, and as far away from Aberdeen as I could get.

A Jubilee Murder

Debbie's prediction that Veronica's house would be "swarming with gendarmes" turned out to be a little wide of the mark. Two pale blue and white panda cars, a plain white Granada and a Bedford ambulance did not even cover half of her driveway. The two ambulancemen sat in the cab, taking long drags on cigarettes, smoke pouring from either window. They could not have looked more bored, clearly unfazed by the famous woman who had just died in that house. Man or woman, rich or poor, it seemed to take a lot more to impress them. As I watched, a cigarette butt was tossed from the drivers' window, trailing a line of smoke down to the gravel where it landed.

The only other sign of life outside the building was a single policeman, who seemed to be patrolling the perimeter and preventing ghoulish members of the public – e.g. Debbie and me – from getting a peek inside the house. The constable had a neatly styled mop of ginger hair and a jaw so square you could use it as a ruler. He was also tall. Ridiculously tall. Neck-achingly tall, when you're only five foot five. But the blue eyes made it worth the effort to look. He also had absolutely huge hands, like two pinky-white frying pans with chubby sausage fingers.

I took off my sunglasses as he approached, but within seconds I knew that this had been a mistake. They were my favourites, plastic tortoiseshell rims with huge graduated brown lenses that all but obscured half of my face. They weren't too dark, but protected my absurdly, mutinously sensitive eyes from the harshness of the sunlight. Until, of course, I took them off. That was when the fun began.

'Afternoon ladies,' the policeman said brightly, in a much less sombre tone than I would've thought appropriate, given the circumstances. 'Are you friends with Miss Castle?'

I recognised the constable. He was our local bobby, whose responsibility were the three villages of Downscliffe, Priory Green and Reydon. But could I remember his name? No, of course not. God forbid, I should recall that minor detail when I really needed it.

'Afternoon Constable…' I ventured, with what I hoped was a winning smile, but probably looked more like I was in a gurning contest. This was the point that my terrible affliction became apparent. One hint of naked sunshine, or indeed any sudden bright light, would have me sneezing uncontrollably for minutes at a time, and this was precisely what happened here. It was a most annoying condition, not to mention highly embarrassing when you're trying not to make a complete numptie of yourself. My face started to contort itself as I felt the first sneeze approach.

'Cropper,' he replied. 'PC Colin Cropper.' He removed his peaked cap with its Sillitoe tartan band and tucked it under his arm, looking at me with curiosity and a modicum of alarm.

'Achoo! Sorry,' I spluttered, 'I just have this…' I sneezed again. And again. I clamped my sunglasses firmly back on my face and grabbed a tissue from my pocket, three more sneezes following in quick succession.

'Don't worry, she often does this,' Debbie explained.

'Achoo!'

'I think she actually does it for attention.'

'Achoo!' With a final, thoroughly humiliated blow of my nose I had recovered sufficiently to rejoin humanity.

'Are you done?' Debbie enquired.

'Ugh. All done. Sorry.' I wiped my nose again and dabbed at the tears welling under my sunglasses. I took a few deep breaths to calm myself, assuming that I had eyeliner smeared over half my face, but by this point just happy to have the sunglasses back in place. 'It's called photic sneeze reflex. One hint of a sunny day and I'm off.'

'Of course, madam. Completely understandable.' There was a hint of a smile threatening to break out across his face, which did nothing to make me feel any better.

'Photic sneeze reflex is one phrase to describe it,' I explained as I continued to dab tears from my eyes. 'Some bright spark of a research scientist with too much time on their hands also called it Autosomal Dominant Compelling Helio-Ophthalmic Outburst. Or ACHOO syndrome for short.'

His lips suddenly went rigid as he tried not to laugh.

'Constable Cropper, you say?' I asked, eager to move things past the unfortunate photic sneezing incident (I was absolutely *not* going to call it ACHOO syndrome). Now I remembered. Cropper the copper. How could I have ever forgotten that? Out of the corner of my eye, I saw Debbie's lips purse and her face contort into a strained grimace. Clearly, she had thought the same thing at the same moment.

'Aye, sorry. PC Cropper. Now I remember. Is there any news?' I asked, trying to move things back to the purpose of our visit here. *Don't think Cropper the copper*; *don't think Cropper the copper*, I repeated in my head, and I tried to ignore the sunshine that crept around the rim of my sunglasses.

'Well, I don't know if you ladies are aware, but Miss Castle was found dead by a neighbour this afternoon. It appears that she's committed suicide. I'm sorry, were you friends?'

As he spoke, the front door opened and a man emerged wearing a blue striped tie and dark suit. In the instant before the door closed again, I caught the briefest glimpse of another figure. My heart began to pound in my chest as I realised this was Veronica, her toes dangling a couple of feet above the ground. She was still wearing the polka dot red dress and expensive white sandals. That was all I could make out before the door slammed shut again. I shot a glance at Debbie and from her parted lips and wide eyes, could tell she had seen it too.

'Not really friends,' I replied. 'At least, not close.' I thought it prudent not to mention that if she had planned to shoot herself, I would have happily supplied the bullets.

'It's a sad business, Mrs…?' He fished in his pocket and withdrew a small black notebook, and plucked a pencil from within its spine. The "Mrs" prefix was probably more than merely a guess, as I still wore a wedding ring on my finger.

'Cameron. Catriona Cameron. That's Catriona with an 'o'. I live at Frisky Pigeons, about a dozen doors down.

'So, K-O-T-R-I-N-A?'

'No,' I laughed. He was clearly not used to dealing with Caledonian nomenclature. 'C-A-T-R-I-O-N-A. But it is pronounced Katrina, and this is my friend, Deborah Dugdale.'

'Pleasure, ladies. It's a real tragedy. My mum watches Miss Castle on the telly. At least, she did. Very sad. She's going to be awfully upset when she hears that she's died. And to hang herself like that?' He shook his head glumly.

'So you're sure it was a suicide, then?' I enquired.

'Oh yes, madam. CID are still inside, but they believe the lady tragically took her own life. We're still waiting for the pathologist to get here. I take it neither of you had any inkling that she was planning this?'

'No officer,' Debbie slurred, and it was only now that I realised she was a little more tiddly than she had seemed back at Frisky Pigeons. Fresh air and alcohol could have that effect, and my tattie wine was perhaps a little more potent than I had given it credit for. 'Like Caty said, we weren't really friends. Veronica was a bit snooty for my taste. Not like Caty. She's common as muck once you get to know her.'

'Yeah, thanks quine.'

'Any time.'

'But neither of us would wish her ill,' I blurted, feeling a little concerned that if foul play was suspected, that we would be positioning ourselves as prime suspects. It would be just typical if we ended up with our photofits on Police 5, with Shaw Taylor doing that funny pointy gesture and warning the public to "keep 'em peeled" for us. I also needed to find some way of shutting Debbie up, before she got us both arrested.

'Oh, I'm sure, madam. Like I said, there doesn't appear to be anything untoward about this case. Just the tragic loss of a young woman's life.'

Young, I thought? That was stretching it a bit. Underneath the make-up that Veronica habitually plastered on her face, probably with a bricklayer's trowel, she had clearly been hurtling toward fifty. 'Aye, tragic, tragic,' I agreed, glancing at my watch. 'Well we really need to be going. I have to pick the kids up from school.'

'If you think you're in a fit state, madam. If you like, I could pick them up for you. I'm sure CID wouldn't miss me for a few minutes.'

It took me a few moments to cotton onto what he meant. 'Aw naw, I knew I'd be driving so stuck to fruity juice. I'm not the alcy-broon around here.' I cast a brief glance in Debbie's direction.

'Of course,' he said with a smile and a nod, positioning the peaked cap on his head again and adjusting it.

'Bye Constable. Thanks for being so gracious.'

'Good day, ladies,' he replied, and turned back

toward the house.

Debbie locked her arm into mine, partly as a sign of affection, but I suspected more to do with ensuring she remained perpendicular. Veronica's house was near the top of Ashfield Lane, and from this vantage point I could just glimpse the tower of the church and the golden cockerel weathervane protruding from the stubby spire. As we walked, it was slowly lost in the shimmering leaves of the cornfield, which swayed back and forth in the light breeze like the waves that I had grown up watching in Aberdeen. In the distance was the soft rumble of traffic on the M20 motorway, mostly lorries trundling back and forth to the continent and cars headed for Maidstone and Ashford. From the field beyond the church came the clattering of a tractor, accompanied by swirling flocks of gulls that circled overhead and swooped down to plunder the upturned earth.

'Nice chap,' Debbie said, her voice clearer and stronger now that the effects of the tattie wine were wearing off a little. 'For a cropper, anyway. Copper the Cropper.'

'Or Cropper the copper, perhaps?' I corrected her. 'Although I wouldn't recommend saying that to his face. There was one interesting thing back there. Did you notice what was missing?

She was silent for a few seconds, until the penny dropped. 'The car?'

'Aye, exactly. What's the betting it's still parked up down at the church?'

'But in that case, how did Veronica get home?'

'That's the big question, isn't it? If she was suicidal, I just can't imagine her traipsing across the field in heels, can you? And why was she in such a hurry when I was talking to Mrs Popplewell? She couldn't wait to get past, as if there was something she desperately needed to be at the church for.'

'You didn't mention this to the constable. Don't you trust him?'

'Of course I do, as much as I'd trust any copper. But I'd probably come across as a bored and slightly neurotic country woman looking for something that isn't there, and for all I know, I very well could be.'

'No, there is something odd about this,' Debbie agreed, coming to a stop. We had arrived at Frisky Pigeons, and her house was a few doors further down. 'Anyway, I'll have to love you and leave you. You've got to pick up the kids, and I've got to create some masterpiece in the kitchen for Lucifer and Beelzebub.'

I stifled a grin as I glanced at my watch. Debbie did love her twin boys really, although anyone would be forgiven if they believed otherwise, with the colourful ways she found to describe them. I saw that it was now a quarter past three, so I couldn't hang about any longer. I didn't like Fergus being out on his own at the best of times, but now, after such a strange day, I was even more protective of him and wanted to be at the school gates when he emerged.

'Fancy a trip into Swanhurst tomorrow?' I asked.

'Sure. Have to be in the morning, though. Tony's got the afternoon off and we're going to Knole Park. With luck, two hours of running around will wear the little horrors out so Tony and me can have a bit of *us* time.' She ended the statement with a cheeky wink, just in case I didn't understand what "us time" meant. I did. Subtlety was not exactly Debbie's forte. It hadn't been *that* long since I'd had some "us time" with a man. I decided against doing the mental arithmetic as I knew all too well that it had indeed been a while.

'Okey dokey, I'll drop the kids off and wait until I see they're indoors.'

'Cheerio,' Debbie said with a smile and a carefree wave as she ambled unsteadily down the lane.

Four

ownscliffe Church of England Primary School was barely a hundred yards from where I had been accosted that morning by Mrs Popplewell. There were only seventy children here, all between the ages of five and eleven. It should have been idyllic, but it was also cliquey, just like the rest of the village. I wondered how many years would drift by before Fergus and I were accepted as villagers, and not in-aboot comers. Considering my accent, probably never.

The fact that I was a very, very, very minor celebrity helped a little, and I was frequently approached by mothers looking for baking tips, wanting to learn about the life of a modern seventies cookbook author, or showing me some wonderful new recipe they had discovered. Alas, most of these were just variations on a theme, and were rarely genuinely novel. However, it did allow me to join, albeit tangentially, the various cliques and covens that blockaded the school gates like a latter-day siege of Troy every afternoon. They were happy to accept an author as an acquaintance, but wished to keep the strange Scottish woman at arms' length. Except Debbie. There had never been any pretence with her. She accepted me at face value without any guile, and I had been more than happy to reciprocate.

I parked Ernie up outside the school at twenty-five past three, one of a dozen or more cars waiting for children to come charging through the school gates. The building itself was a single-storey structure, the upper half clad in white-painted timber. Next door was the village hall where the kids would endure PE lessons, put on atrocious theatrical presentations (school plays were always atrocious and no one is ever going to convince me otherwise) and was the venue for more adult oriented functions, like fortnightly dances, jumble sales and acting as the local polling station whenever it was time to elect a new bunch of clueless numpties.

As usual, there were gaggles of parents, almost all of whom were women. The tiny handful of men would huddle together in tight groups for mutual protection. Some of the women stood silently, pensive and waiting to be called upon to speak. Others stood back, arms folded across their chests and nodding emphatically when one of the groups' seniors – and every group had one – made a statement or demand with which they fervently agreed. I was never good at being a member of these little cabals, probably because, by nature, I rarely agreed wholeheartedly with anyone about anything.

A Three Villages Mystery

'Catriona, have you heard?' a voice yelled. I didn't even need to look around to see who it was. Barbara Johnson had a voice that could curdle fresh milk, and was impossible to ignore no matter how hard I might try. I looked round and there she was, wearing a long faux-tweed skirt and cream turtleneck jumper. Her brown shoes were matronly and eminently practical, and I couldn't envisage her ever trying something a little more adventurous, although I was hardly in a position to pass judgement. I was still wearing my denim dungarees with flowery patches, rock god David Bowie t-shirt, and white plimmies.

'Hi Barbara,' I replied loudly, hoping to be heard over the excited hubbub. The gossip seemed to be more animated than usual, and I guessed that by now, news of Veronica Castle's untimely demise had spread like a shockwave through the home counties. 'Do you mean about Veronica?'

'Of course, duck. Unless you know of any other famous people who died today?'

'I reckon she was in a lot of debt,' one of the other girls stated quite fervently, absently flapping one flared trouser leg against the other. 'That's why she killed herself.'

'She *was* a bit of a drama queen,' said another, fanning herself with a copy of Woman's Weekly. 'I wonder if she was jilted by a fella, maybe?'

'Which one?' asked another, and there was general muted chortling.

'Oh, I most seriously doubt that was the reason,' Barbara countered. 'Not a sentimental bone in that woman's body. Hardly the type to sulk for long, let alone top herself.'

'I have it on good authority,' said yet another with her hair tied up in a tight bun, and who wore some fearsome horn-rimmed spectacles, 'that her TV contract was about to be cancelled.'

'No, really?'

'On my life.'

In a different situation, this ardent exchange might have been quite funny. No, I did not like Veronica Castle in the slightest, but the woman had just died and her body wouldn't even be cold yet. Whatever the circumstances, I thought she deserved a little more respect than to have her life publicly picked apart in this way. Still, there's nowt so queer as folk, and I wasn't about to question them. I did wonder whether any of them might, however inadvertently, stumble onto the truth – or at least a version of it.

My musings and the gossip were cut short as there was the rattle and crash of a door flying open, followed an instant later by the jubilant cries of a small but extremely vocal tidal wave of five to eleven-year-olds as they exploded from the confines of the school. A surge of running, screaming children poured through the gate and toward gleeful mothers, brandishing garish paintings, satchels and duffel bags bouncing on their shoulders. As irrational as it was, I always – always – felt a wave of relief when I saw Fergus among them, safe, happy and excited. I spied him through the churning throng, a brightly-coloured painting clutched in one hand, waving it at me like a prize won fiercely in battle.

'Mum! Mum,' he shouted, and a second later, he crashed into me with all the grace of a piano being dropped out of a second-storey window.

He took a moment to fling his arms around me, burying his head in my stomach. I reciprocated, holding my baby tight until I felt him begin to wriggle free. The greatest things in the world were cuddles from my little boy, and the worst feeling of all was letting him go.

'Mum, look what I did,' he said, an ecstatic beaming grin plastered across his face.

I took the sheet from him and held it up to look at it. It took a few seconds to register that I had it upside down, so turned it over. Apparently I was supposed to instinctively know that in Fergus's imaginary world, the sky was green and the land was orange. The blue box in the middle should have been a clue.

'Oh, what a surprise,' I teased. 'Doctor Who. You never feel the urge to knock out a Turner seascape or a Constable?'

'Constable who?' he asked with an earnest frown.

I rolled my eyes heavenward and pointed at Ernie. 'Come on, Rembrandt, get in.' I always parked with the passenger door next to the pavement when picking the boys up. Freddie and Arthur, Debbie's "Lucifer and Beelzebub", piled in the back, and Fergus sat in the front with me.

The five-minute drive back to Ashfield Lane was a raucous affair, three ten-year-old boys making enough noise to wake the dead. I winced at the expression, realising that it was an unfortunate turn of phrase on this occasion. But it did remind me to glance across to the church as we went past. Sure enough, the little red sports car was still there, parked up on the grass verge next to the church gate.

'Hey, twins from hell,' I shouted, and they went quiet, sniggering away in the back. 'I'm going to drop you home, but I'll wait until you're safe and sound indoors. Okay? Go straight in and no loitering about outside.'

'Okay Auntie Catriona, but we're not kids, you know.'

'Just for now. There might be something going on, and me and your mum want to make sure you're both safe. Do me a favour and just go straight indoors, you hear? No messing aboot or I'll skelp your bahookies.'

There were grumbles of acceptance and a minute later, Ernie pulled up outside Debbie's house, and all three boys poured out of the car. I watched the twins run down the front path (these boys never seemed to do anything at less than full throttle) and waited until I saw the door open and Debbie wave frantically back like a mad woman.

'I'll drop you home, Fergs,' I said, pulling up to our driveway and manoeuvring to reverse in. 'Then I need to go out for a few minutes. Can you let yourself in?'

'Okay Mum,' he replied, more focused on his picture

than on me.

'Have you got your key?'

He rummaged in his pocket, pulling out a Space 1999 keyring, as well as a couple of orange Space Dust wrappers. 'Right here,' he said, waggling the jingling keys in front of my face.

'Good. I'll wait until you're inside, and don't answer the door to anyone while I'm out.'

'Not even you, Mum?'

'I've got a key, smart Alec.'

He chuckled, apparently feeling quite pleased with himself.

'Have you had any other ideas about the fancy dress for the jubilee?'

'A Dalek,' he replied, not missing a beat.

'Anything that's *not* a Dalek.'

'Umm… The Doctor?'

The Doctor, I thought. Now that was a possibility. A long coat, a scarf, a big hat, and I wouldn't have to sacrifice my sink plunger. How hard could that be? 'Okay, I'll see what I can do. Now g'way you go.' I leaned across and gave him a kiss before he scrambled from the car, vaulted the low wrought iron fence Adam West Batman style, and ran to the door, disappearing inside.

'My son, the bohemian,' I mused with a chuckle, before driving off again and wondering how come a ten-year-old could get the door open first try and I couldn't.

Five

wo minutes after dropping Fergus home, I pulled up outside the church and, sure enough, there was Veronica's car still parked on the grass verge, under the yew trees that offered the church some protection from the cricket pitch. On one side were farm buildings, and on the other a single seventeenth century cottage. The property's brickwork was a rust-red higgledy-piggledy mess, numerous areas having been patched over the centuries, while its tiled roof rose and dipped like waves on the ocean frozen in time.

Rumour had it the house was haunted. A man had been murdered there, so the legend went, sometime in the murky past. It was said he could sometimes be seen at an upstairs window, awaiting his doom. Years later, the family dog had allegedly seen the ghost and leapt, terrified, from the window to die on the unyielding ground below. Now they haunted the place together, apparitions from different times. What I never understood was how they knew the dog had seen the man's ghost. Had it left a note before hurling itself from the upstairs window? Or miraculously gained the power of speech and shouted, "Oh no, it's a ghost!" before plunging into oblivion? Who knew? Maybe it was just barking.

I muttered a curse under my breath as I realised I was not completely alone here. The front door to the cottage was open and the lady of the house, a frightfully posh and exceptionally dopey specimen called Celia Fernsby-Brown, stood there in her dressing gown. I checked my watch, just to make sure I hadn't gone completely potty, and confirmed that it really was just after four in the afternoon. Celia was being doorstepped by a stout looking woman in a wax jacket and wellies, clasping a ramblers' walking stick like she was about to take it into battle. Celia waved over to me, a big cheesy grin on her face, eyes as blissfully vacant as ever, and continued chatting to her visitor. I waved back and headed for the church gate. Everyone who knew me, knew that I had no relatives in the area, so I was unlikely to be visiting the grave of a loved one. My excuse for any such situation was to say that I was on the hunt for wild herbs, which sounded plausible enough, I thought.

There was one other car parked on the verge, an old Morris Minor in a faded black that had long since lost its sheen, complete with a bubbly rust trim around the door edges and wheel arches. Several of the chirruping birds in the yew trees overhead had left little messages on the car's roof, and one had scored a direct hit on the windscreen, which had splattered over the glass like a fried egg. Everyone in the village knew the car of Reverend Cackett. He was an eccentric, to say the least, and puritanical, even by the standards of the Anglican church. He was not exactly stern and scary in the traditional bible thumping, fire breathing manner of the ecclesiastical archetype, but I certainly found any conversation with him to be an unnerving experience. He was tall and rangy, the top of his head bald and shiny like polished chrome, his dark hair having retreated to the sides and back where it was Brylcreemed into place.

The church itself was ancient, the original building dating from the twelfth century, the tower being added much later. Like so many country churches, it appeared to be sunken into the ground, as if the Earth was trying to drag it beneath the surface. But, like all those other buildings, the clue was in its function and, more crucially, what surrounded it. Gravestones jutted out of the ground at a variety of angles. Those surrounding the entrance were old, some dating back to the eighteenth century, their faces covered in moss and the stonework crumbling as time began to defeat them. With an unhurried destructiveness, lichens drilled into the granite and obliterated the words that had been so painstakingly carved. Eventually the headstones would be quietly replaced. This, naturally, had happened repeatedly over the centuries, the original bodies left in place, piled one atop the other. There were around a hundred gravestones in the churchyard by my estimation, but that did not mean there were a hundred bodies buried here. The parish had a population of around five hundred people, a figure that had remained remarkably static over the centuries, as was attested to by Downscliffe's entry in the Domesday Book of 1086 AD. The number of corpses that lay beneath the exceptionally lush grass was probably closer to a quite inconceivable forty thousand. Possibly a lot more, as this could well have been a place of worship and interment for hundreds or even thousands of years before that.

It was peaceful here, as churchyards so often are. Some people might find it creepy, but I was often never more relaxed than when spending time among the dead like this, wandering around and reading the scant snippets of people's lives on the gravestones. It wasn't always easy. Some were lovingly tended, fresh flowers arranged carefully in memorial vases. Others were just left, and I wondered if they ever received any visitors at all. Some were hidden in the willow and sycamore trees whose branches hung low, almost brushing the ground like a death shroud of mottled greens.

In the distance, I heard the rattle of an ill-fitting old door close, and hoped the coast would be clear. As relaxing as it was being in this graveyard, I was anxious not to get caught by Reverend Cackett, and at the back of my mind I thought of Fergus being alone in the house. Casting a furtive look back at the church, I made sure there was no sign of the vicar emerging from the arched entrance. It looked like I would get away with it.

Veronica's car had been neatly reversed onto the

grassy verge, between two yew trees. I kept telling myself that I was reading too much into things, that she had simply killed herself because of whatever personal demons that had been tormenting her. There was very little about this business that was genuinely suspicious, and my overactive imagination had, on occasion, caused me to exaggerate the perceived negatives in a situation. But there was something about this that seemed different, certain pieces of the puzzle that did not fit as they should. The way the car was parked was one of these things. It was too neat. I had no idea how a suicidal woman should feel, but would she have taken such care with her parking if she were about to end it all? Why had she been in such a hurry to get to the church, and then left her car behind to trudge uphill across a field, and then still have another hundred yards to walk up the road. Come to think of it, it's amazing that no one saw her. Then again, maybe they did. Maybe it was just me who wasn't paying much attention.

There didn't seem to be anything terribly special about the car, aside from the fact that it was a little red Triumph roadster. It was an 'N' reg, built in 1974. I found it mildly surprising that Veronica didn't have a personalised plate. She was certainly vain enough not to want people to know that she drove around in a three-year-old car. It was a soft top, but she had left the roof down when she parked the car. There were already scraps of dead leaves and fragments of bark dropping onto the cream leather seats. Aside from the fresh fall of detritus from the yew tree above, the interior was quite immaculate with nothing of interest to see. She must have taken her handbag with her, and the glove compartment was an open style, with nothing inside but a few lipstick-stained tissues. I didn't want to physically touch anything. If the police did decide belatedly that this was a suspicious death, I didn't want my fingerprints all over the dead woman's car. It was an uncomfortable fact that I would be, if not the prime suspect, then certainly under suspicion. That damning review of my bread puddings might be motive enough for the police.

I filched around in my pockets for something to cover my hand with. I fished out a small handkerchief with embroidered flower patterns at two corners, and reached under the driver's seat to rummage around. There were more tissues under there, and a small cylinder which was quickly revealed to be a scarlet lipstick. I reached in a little deeper, pushing my hankie-covered fingers through more tissues, until I felt something else. It wasn't tissue, but a small shred of paper.

'This ain't your car, Miss,' came an emotionless male voice from behind me.

I froze, suddenly abundantly aware that I had been caught completely red handed. My fingers closed around first the piece of paper, and then the lipstick. Straightening up, I made a show of brushing myself down, and surreptitiously slipped the paper into my pocket as I did so.

'Got it!' I declared triumphantly, holding aloft a

grubby, dust coated lipstick. I caught my first glimpse of the man, wearing a tattered check shirt unbuttoned halfway to his belly button, faded and ripped bell-bottomed jeans, and a pair of boots so caked in dried mud that I couldn't tell you their original colour if you held a gun to my head. His hair was dark, with bushy sideburns ending not far shy of his chin. And then there was the smell; this man clearly had not been introduced to the delights of antiperspirant deodorant. I recognised him as one of the local tractor drivers, and surmised he must be the one who had been working the field adjacent to the church. I'm quick like that. He was also notable as being the only one in the village with his very own observatory in the back garden. I could actually see his house from my front window, the observatory a gleaming white dome at the foot of the North Downs. If he studied the stars in his spare time, then he was probably somewhat smarter than his appearance suggested, so it would be best not to underestimate him.

'That's your make-up, Miss?' he asked dubiously, staring at the lipstick, tufts of claggy dust clinging to the scarlet gel.

· 'Aye, it just fell out of my pooch as I was leaning inside. Isn't this a beautiful car?' I gushed. 'I've never seen one of these up close and just *had* to have a look. Do you know whose car it is?'

He seemed quite taken aback by my excitement, and took half a step back from the crazy woman. 'That be the car of Miss Veronica. Veronica Castle. You know, the food lady.'

'Oh, Veronica Castle. This is her car? That would make sense.'

'Would it?'

'Well, I wouldn't expect a celebrity like her to drive around in an old heap like mine.' I gestured with a flick of my head toward the crumbling old Escort, and whispered a silent apology to Ernie.

'I suppose not. Have you heard about her, Miss…?'

'Only her television programme,' I replied a little evasively, trying to deflect the enquiry. 'I'm not an avid viewer, but I catch the odd episode.'

'No, no, no. I meant, have you heard that she's dead?'

'G'way ye go!'

'Oh yes, Miss. Died today, as far as I'm understanding. Hanged herself, she did.'

'Well, I never. It makes you think, doesn't it? I suppose money cannae always buy you happiness.'

'I suppose not, Miss. I was thinking I should probably call the old bill; let them know where Miss Castle's car is?'

'I'd say that was a good idea. Anyway, I really must be going now,' I said, pocketing the lipstick and turning toward Ernie.

'Can I ask your name, Miss?' he shouted after me. 'Just in case the old bill ask?'

I sighed inwardly, realising there was no way I could get out of it.

'Catriona,' I shouted back and waved, opening the door as fast as I could and slipping inside.

I couldn't give a false name, could I? Oh no, that would be far too easy. No, brains here didn't think of actually lying. I can be really, really dopey sometimes. Dopey enough to give Celia Fernsby-Brown a run for her money in a brainless of Britain contest. Then again, if I gave him a false name, what if he noted Ernie's licence plate? The police might find it suspicious if I lied about my identity when caught prying in a dead woman's car. It seemed honesty was not just the best policy, but sadly the only alternative.

Ernie clearly hadn't taken offence at the "old heap" comment, and his engine fired into life at the second time of asking, which was good for him. 'Good boy, Ernie,' I whispered, patting the steering wheel lightly.

I nearly screamed when I looked round, and saw the tractor driver's face almost pressed against my side window. He gestured with a rolling motion for me to lower it, and I had a sudden and uncomfortable realisation that I was in an extremely vulnerable position. I'm sure what little colour there had been in my face had immediately drained away. What if *he* was the murderer? What if he thought that I had seen too much? What if I was to be his next victim? I'd seen The Sweeney and Van der Valk, and knew how these things played out. Initially, I had been concerned that I was acting suspiciously; now I was concerned for my life. If I opened the window, all he would have to do was reach in and grab my throat.

But what choice did I have? So, slowly and reluctantly, I did as he wished, and rolled the window down.

'Catriona what, Miss?' he asked, his face close enough for me to smell his breath. I didn't want his breath to be the last thing I smelled. Or his intrusive armpits.

'Cameron,' I mumbled. 'Catriona Cameron. And your name is?'

He stared at me for a moment, as if sizing me up; considering what my motives might be. Pondering whether to kill me, perhaps? 'Why would you want to know my name, Miss Catriona?'

'I… I like to know who I'm dealing with. And you never know, the police might want to talk to me as well. They often do in these situations, don't they?' I made a show of putting the car into reverse. I wanted to let this character know that I was ready to leave as soon as he'd divulged his name. Or make a quick getaway, should I have to.

He contemplated this for an uncomfortably long moment before nodding. 'Fair enough, Miss Catriona. I'm Barry Huckstep, tractor driver and farm hand for Wimble's Farm, just in case the old bill want to know who I am.'

'Thank you,' I smiled, hoping it didn't look like a terrified grimace. 'I'll see you around, Barry.'

I slowly reversed back off the grass verge, trying to keep things as calm and natural as I could, and pulled away. I didn't relax until I was back home, Ernie was in the garage and I was safely indoors with Fergus.

Barry Huckstep was just about the creepiest individual I had met since moving to Kent, with the possible exception of Reverend Cackett. No, even creepier than him, I decided. I rummaged in my pocket and felt the manky old lipstick, my thumb and forefinger now caked in scarlet goo. This day was just getting better and better. The sticky fingers closed around the piece of paper and I withdrew it to finally be able to study the small sheet in more detail.

Initially, I could not have been more disappointed. The mysterious piece of paper was just a till receipt. There was no name to identify where it had come from, just a date and the value of whatever had been bought.

'That you Mum?' came a yell from Fergus's bedroom. In the background I could hear the electronic boop-boop-beep-biddly-boop of his Binatone Pong game, and an episode of Thunderbirds on audiotape. Fergus had dozens and dozens of his favourite television programmes on C90 cassette, everything from Thunderbirds and Space 1999 to Logan's Run and Man from Atlantis. His room was a minefield of toys, just waiting to maim a barefooted mother inadvertently wandering in.

'Aye, only me, loon,' I yelled back. Indoors and alone, we generally reverted to speaking in the Aberdonian dialect that we had both grown up using. But even so, it saddened me a little to note that Fergus was slowly losing his accent, assimilating the southern English vernacular to which he was constantly exposed these days.

'What's for tea?'

'Don't know, I haven't caught it yet.'

I turned the piece of paper over in my hand, the sheet feeling slightly damp in my fingers, and on the back were a handful of letters, hand-written in blue biro: T. WILLS. I pulled the lopsided gurning expression I always did when first presented with a puzzle. T. WILLS? Was that a name? Or perhaps a hint at an occupation? Maybe a solicitor, I mused, that specialised in wills? A solicitor with a name beginning with "T" perhaps? There were dozens, perhaps hundreds of possible explanations, and the chances were that it had nothing to do with Veronica's death.

There was one person who might be able to shed a little more light on things, and since I was going to be in the neighbourhood tomorrow anyway, it wouldn't do any harm to give him a quick call.

The house phone was in the hall, which was probably the worst possible place for it. The phone itself was a standard GPO wall mounted telephone, in dreary two-tone grey with a dial. One day, I promised myself, I would get a snazzy push button unit, but this would have to do for now until I was properly settled.

I flicked open my phone book, the pages covered in hastily scrawled numbers, many of which had been embellished with swirling doodles as I had talked to people. The corners were tattered, and most of the tabs curled over. I first went to the 'C' tab, but there was nothing of any help there. Then I tried the 'P' tab, and that was where I found it. There were three numbers listed. The first was '999', circled in garish red pen. This was for Fergus's benefit, should there ever be an emergency. The second was the local station's number in Swanhurst, where Debbie and I were going tomorrow. The third was listed as "PC Colin Cropper – local bobby". It was oddly pleasing to me that nearly a century-and-a-half after Robert Peel had formed the Metropolitan Police Force, they were still called "bobbies" in his honour.

Telephones with dials always hurt my fingers, so I used the barrel of a pen to dial. After three rings, it was answered by a switchboard operator.

'Hello, Swanhurst Police. Can I help you?' It was a woman, with the kind of no-nonsense tone that did not encourage banter or waffle. It probably didn't help that it was late on a Friday afternoon, and she was either looking forward to going home, or really not looking forward to a rowdy Friday night at the station.

'Hi, my name's Catriona Cameron. Would it be possible to speak to PC Cropper, please?' I winced at the sound of my own simpering voice, which to me sounded like Oliver Twist asking for some more lovely gruel.

'Just a moment; I'll see if he's still here. He might have gone home for the day.'

'That's okay, I don't mind waiting while you—' I didn't get to finish the sentence, the woman disappearing, to be replaced by a series of rhythmic beeps. After maybe fifteen seconds, I heard a ringing tone again, and the electronically modified voice of PC Cropper. Cropper the copper himself.

'Colin Cropper,' he said simply.

'Hello. I wonder if you remember me. We spoke earlier outside Veronica Castle's house? I was with my friend.'

'Oh yes, it was…' I heard the rustle of a piece of paper, and smiled as I heard him hurriedly consulting his notebook. Clearly, I had made quite an impression on him. So much so that he had forgotten my name already. 'Mrs Cameron? You were with your mildly sozzled friend.'

'That was us. I was wondering if we could meet up tomorrow morning? I've had some thoughts on Veronica's death, and to be honest, wanted to pick your brains a little.'

'Sure, no problem. Would you like me to come out to Downscliffe, or can you come to the station?'

'Could we meet for coffee perhaps?' I asked, not keen on going to the station. They might not let me out again. Then a horrible thought struck me. He might think I was asking him out on a date! 'I'll have my friend Debbie with me,' I blurted, hoping that might dispel any misconceptions.

'That's fine. The more, the merrier,' he replied, and I could hear the grin in his voice. 'How about we all meet up at Molly's Tea Room. Say, ten in the morning?'

'That'd be braw. Thank you, Constable. Goodnight, enjoy your evening.'

'And you, Mrs Cameron.'

Six

Saturday morning was, as always, accompanied by the dulcet tones of Ed "Stewpot" Stewart presenting Radio One's Junior Choice, with that irritating jingle shouting, "ello darlin", which grated on me every time I heard it. Every time. Without fail.

Debbie called just before eight, mercifully interrupting Terry Scott's rendition of "My Brother", before it moved on to Clive Dunn doddering his way through "Grandad", and then The Wombles imploring everyone to "Remember You're a Womble". I reassured her that yes, we were still on for this morning, and that we had a meeting with PC Cropper at ten.

'You've got a date with Cropper the copper?' she asked with a note of astonished, but decidedly malicious delight.

'It is not a date!' I yelled back, wishing to nip that one in the bud immediately. 'Just a meeting on neutral ground. And you are going to be there, quine, so let's not have any of that nonsense thank you very much.'

A Three Villages Mystery

She hung up, still giggling, and I could tell it was going to be another one of *those* days.

We picked Debbie and the kids up at just after half eight, and ten minutes later, deposited them with Debbie's mum in Reydon, the third of our triumvirate of small Kentish villages. With three squabbling, shouting, shrieking kids squeezed onto Ernie's back seat, and two 'adults' in the front, yelling over the noise, it was like cranking the volume right down on the hi-fi when we could finally kick them all out of the car and continue on to Swanhurst. Don't get me wrong, I loved Fergus more than anything else in the world, and always would, and Debbie felt precisely the same way toward Freddie and Arthur. Okay, she would habitually scream at them that they were the terrible twins, the twin spawn of Satan, or demon children from hell etc. After all, we were in the age of The Exorcist and The Omen, but she wouldn't change them for the world.

But what bliss it was when we could be free for a couple of hours, and have grown up conversations.

'I'm wondering why Bungle, from Rainbow, wears pyjamas to bed, but walks around naked all day,' Debbie pondered as we came off the A20 and made our way into Swanhurst. This, alas, seemed to be her definition of adult conversation. 'I mean, he's covered in fur so it's not really an issue but still, it's an odd thing to do, don't you think?'

'I cannae say I've ever really given it much consideration,' I replied with a shake of my head. 'I'll tell you what I am considering though.'

'What's that?'

'Booking a psychiatrist appointment for you.'

She giggled. 'I can't help it if I think about these things. By the way, you're looking bomb today,' she said, giving me a swift once over.

I frowned. Maybe what I was wearing was a little dressier than usual: three quarter length chequered skirt, a pale lemon cheesecloth blouse, corduroy waistcoat and knee-high boots. Not dungarees, but not exactly hotpants and go-go boots either. 'We have a meeting with a member of the local constabulary. I thought it best to make a good impression.'

'You'll make an impression all right, foxy mama. Are we parking in the big car park?'

'Uh-huh,' I confirmed as I pulled into the big car park just behind the Fresh Fayre supermarket.

Swanhurst was a mishmash of old, not so old and a handful of new buildings. A proper little chocolate box country town nestling in the heart of the Garden of England.

There was a free space in the shade of the laburnums at the far end. It was a sunny day and after a couple of hours out in the open, Ernie would be hot enough inside to bake biscuits. I didn't mind walking the extra few yards, even if Debbie had been known to grumble.

'And don't get me started on Winnie the Pooh,' she continued as I walked around the car, locking both doors. 'I mean I'm all for cardigans, but it's hardly enough to keep your essentials covered in winter, is it?'

A Three Villages Mystery

Yes, definitely one of *those* days.

'What are we actually in town for?' she asked, as her children's television and films existential crisis subsided. 'Apart from your date with Cropper the copper.'

She just *had* to get that little jibe in. 'Well, I'll need to get my messages from Fresh Fayre's for this cake I've been press-ganged into making. You know, the Queen's chocolate biscuit cake?'

'How could I forget? Honestly Caty, why couldn't you just tell old Mrs Popply-whatsit that you didn't want to enter that contest?'

'Because I'd never hear the end of it and be the laughing stock of Downscliffe for all eternity. "Oh look, there goes that Cameron woman – the one who chickened out of baking a cake". That's what they'll all be bletherin' aboot. You can guarantee that Mrs Popplewell would be spreading that kind of stuff if I said no. You know what she's like. In fact, you know what they're *all* like in that village.'

She nodded as we made it onto the High Street. 'Fair point. But have you thought about what would happen if you didn't win? You, the groovy cookbook author?'

'Of course I've thought about it. Especially when I thought Veronica was going to be the judge. Not much chance of that happening now.'

We wandered past Fresh Fayre with its garish crash-bang-wallop signs offering special offers on Ski yogurts, Quosh cordials and Stork SB margarine.

'Let's do the supermarket last,' I said as we passed

the entrance. 'Don't want to be laden down with shopping bags.'

'Okay, aside from Fresh Fayre and Cropper the copper, what else?'

'Charity shops for Fergus's costume.'

'Oh yeah, that's right. I've still got to decide on what Freddie and Arthur are going to wear. I was thinking a pair of Satan's minions, but not sure where to get the forked tails and devil horns. Not that they need fake ones.'

I never failed to chuckle at the way Debbie 'abused' her twins. They were a handful, yes, but not *that* bad. Not really.

'Are we looking for sink plungers and the like, then?' she asked.

'Thankfully, no. Fergus has moderated his ambitions, just a little. So, the Dalek is out, and Doctor Who himself is in.'

'Ah, so we're talking long coat and a long scarf?'

'And a wide-brimmed hat.'

We spent an enjoyable half an hour browsing through the half a dozen charity shops at the north end of the High Street, rummaging through clothing racks and nick-nack boxes. I was lucky enough to find two striped scarves that I could sew together, and a suitable hat. It was a fawny beige colour, but I was fairly sure it could be dyed to a more authentic maroon. Finding a long coat in Fergus's size was more of a challenge. It's always the way; the thing you expect to be easy, turns out to be the most problematic. I did find a woman's double-breasted coat that might fit the bill. As it was, he would look like a camp bookie, but I could shorten it and get rid of the thick, fur-lined collar, and the colour was about right.

'I think we're done here,' I said, clutching two armfuls of clothes and hoping none of them had fleas.

'Really?' Debbie queried. 'I thought he was going as Doctor Who, not Jason King?'

'I can make a few alterations.'

'You'll have to. You could scar the poor kid for life. What about the hair?'

My face fell. 'Oh, I hadn't thought of the hair.'

She glanced at her watch, and I did the same. 'We've got ten minutes until your hot date with Cropper of the Yard. The cat welfare shop usually has a collection of wigs. At least I think they're human wigs and not cat fur. If it says "Mr Tiddles" on the lining, run. We can make it if we're quick.'

'Aye, but it's not a date.'

Molly's Tea Room was on the corner of Queen Street and Western Lane, just off the High Street and secluded enough not to be too busy. The building had originally been painted white, but this had dulled over the years as pollution and the elements had taken their toll. Brown and grey streaks ran down the outer walls. Just outside the window was a colonnade of pillars. This would have been a good place to put half a dozen outdoor tables, but so far the owners had resisted this outrageous concept, possibly because of the vagaries of the British climate, or perhaps because they didn't trust the locals not to run off without paying.

Inside, the tea room was much more pleasant, as long as you didn't mind the blast furnace temperature. Kettles, toasters and ovens generated a lot of heat. In winter it would be described as cosy, but in early June, the temperature was positively oppressive. At least, it was to my Aberdonian sensibilities.

A cloud of steam hung in the air, condensation misting the windows and small rivulets running down the glass. There was a curious mixture of aromas; eggs and bacon mixed with cinnamon and freshly baked pastries and mildly singed toast. Just to complete the tableau, a small transistor radio was playing in the background, the dulcet tones of Kid Jensen being drowned out by the clatter of pans and metal trays.

When we arrived, practically crashing through the doorway, PC Cropper was at the counter, ordering coffee. He looked round and smiled when he saw us, the look turning to one of bemusement as he saw me laden down with a huge secondhand C&A bag of charity shop tat.

'Good morning, ladies,' he greeted us with a grin. 'I've ordered three coffees. Is that okay? Did either of you want a slice of cake?'

I had known he was tall, but in the confined space of the tea room, he seemed positively huge, practically stooped over in the low-ceilinged café.

'Oh no, I'm fine, thanks,' I said, almost knocking an old lady's hat off with my bag as I manoeuvred into the room.

A Three Villages Mystery

'Speak for yourself,' Debbie grumbled. 'I'm always in the mood for cake; why do you think I keep *you* around?'

PC Cropper seemed to find this amusing, and gestured for her to peruse the sweets in the glass cabinet under the counter.

Debbie bent down, studying what was on offer more carefully. I could understand that. Cake was a serious business, and this was a decision not to be taken lightly. She put a finger to her lips for a second as she pondered the choices, and finally made up her mind, pointing at the second shelf down. 'I think I'll have… that one. A rum baba.'

The sticky, doughnut-shaped cake was topped with a dollop of synthetic whipped cream, and was clearly beckoning to her to be chosen. Since she was throwing caution to the wind, I decided to join her. 'On second thoughts, I think I'll try a slice of the banana-pineapple spice cake.' This looked even deadlier than the rum baba, a gooey sponge dotted with spices, and topped with a generous layer of icing and chopped walnuts. I fumbled in my shoulder bag for my purse, but the constable held up a hand.

'Please, my treat.' He handed over a five-pound note and collected his change from the young woman at the till, and we took our seats in the far corner.

'Looks like you've had a busy morning,' PC Cropper noted, pouring a more than generous amount of sugar into his coffee as he eyed my gigantic C&A bag.

A Jubilee Murder

'Ugh, this,' I said with a groan. 'I was hoping not to be quite such a hazard to shipping when we came here, but it's for the jubilee day celebration. Actually, it's my bairn's fancy dress costume.'

'Oh, what's he going as?'

'Doctor Who. He's nuts about it.'

Debbie had already started tucking into her rum baba, and had a blob of cream on the end of her nose. I tried to give the (completely false) impression that I was a little more refined and carved a small piece of my Hummingbird cake off with a dessert fork and tasted it. I hadn't expected it to be a genuinely fine piece, but was mistaken. Hats off to you, Molly, or whoever was responsible for it. I decided it was the best thing to come out of the West Indies since Viv Richards.

'He'd enjoy a trip to Police Headquarters in Hendon, then,' the constable said. 'There's a Tardis outside the main entrance. Actually it's a genuine police box, but to his generation, it's a Tardis.'

'Is it still in use?' I asked, once I'd gulped a mouthful of cake. I was looking far less elegant and dignified than I wanted to, but the cake was just too good.

'No, there probably wouldn't be much use for a working police box, right outside police headquarters. They have cells inside, you know.'

I shrugged. 'Fair point.' I passed a napkin to Debbie. 'Nose.'

'Oops. Sorry,' she said, sucking rum syrup from her fingers.

A Three Villages Mystery

I had happily polished off three quarters of my slice of cake, but set my fork down sadly, deciding that I ought to leave the rest and try not to look a total pig.

'You two looked like you enjoyed those,' he said with two raised ginger eyebrows.

'Oh, you have no idea,' Debbie replied, gazing at the last of the rum juice on the plate and clearly looking like she wanted to scoop it up with her finger, or go the whole hog and just lick the plate clean.

'Now, I was wondering why you'd asked to meet me today?' he said, before taking a tentative sip of his steaming coffee.

'Ah, that. Aye. Is Veronica's death still being treated as a suicide?'

'It is. CID were confident nothing untoward had been going on. At least, there were no others involved. I think suicide is untoward enough.'

'What about her car?' I asked, and that seemed to garner his attention.

'Her car?'

'Aye, it wasn't at her house yesterday.'

'No, it was reported to us this morning, first thing. It looks like it had been sat outside the church all night. I think it'll be towed back to the property later today.'

'Aye, I saw it as I drove past yesterday, not long before she died. I thought it was odd then, but didn't think about it anymore until Debbie brought me the news.'

'I see,' he said, extracting his notebook from a pocket and beginning to write. 'What time did you see it?'

'I'd say the back of one.'

He looked up with a frown. 'The back of…?'

'After one in the afternoon. I'd just been talking to Mrs Popplewell. I don't actually know *her* first name. She'd flagged me down to talk about the jubilee, and Veronica had driven past. In fact, she seemed to be in quite a hurry. A couple of minutes later I saw her car parked outside the church.'

'I see,' he muttered after a moment, once he had translated my words in his head. He scribbled the bare facts into the book. 'Well, I can inform CID of this, but frankly, in my experience, it would have to be something a bit more concrete to get them to reopen enquiries.'

'But do you think it's significant?' I pressed.

'Maybe; maybe not. I think she might have just been a very unhappy lady. Of course, something could well have tipped her over the edge, but that doesn't mean anyone else was to blame. At least, not in the eyes of the law.'

This was, unfortunately, precisely what I'd expected. It wasn't his fault. He was just a lowly local bobby, and his powers were limited.

'I, er… I did go and have a look at her car yesterday afternoon. After we'd spoken to you.'

His head sagged and he let out a long sigh. 'And you didn't report it?'

'I didn't think there was much to report,' I whispered in a conspiratorial tone, wondering why I was doing it and who might be involved in our conspiracy. 'I didn't actually touch the car, Constable, so dinna fash yersel'.'

He shook his head. 'Call me Colin. Now, I don't want you going around like Nancy Drew investigating this yourself, you hear me? If there's any investigating to be done, leave it to the police. It's sort of what we're here for.'

'But there's not any investigating being done, Con— Colin.'

He shrugged and spread his huge hands in a "sorry, nothing I can do" gesture. 'That's the way it is, Mrs Cameron.'

'Call me Catriona,' I said, and gave him a small smile.

'And you can call me Debbie,' came another voice, not wanting to be too left out.

'There was one other thing,' I ventured. 'When I went to look at the car at the church, there was a man there – a local tractor driver. He was acting very strange. It was actually quite intimidating.'

'Do you know his name?'

'He said it was Barry Huckstep. He works at Wimble's Farm.'

'Okay, I'll follow this up. Maybe have a word with him and tell him not to go around scaring the ladies.' He accompanied this statement with a mischievous wink.

'Is there any chance you can let us into her hoose?' I asked, and instantly had my answer.

'Veronica Castle's? Are you completely bonkers? Absolutely not. Seriously, do not go down that route.'

'But you said there's no investigation going on.'

'I know, but you're talking about criminal trespass. At the very least.'

'So, bad idea then?'

He rolled his eyes heavenward. 'About as bad as you could have.' He leaned forward, clasping his thick, sausage-like fingers together. 'Look, I'll take what you told me to CID and see what they say, but I don't hold out too much hope. Now…' He looked at his watch. 'I'm afraid I have to be going. Being the local copper for three villages is more work than you might realise.'

'Oh, I can imagine,' I said, feeling a little deflated by the meeting. Had I been ticked off for overstepping the mark? Clearly, yes, and that stung a little. I deserved it, to be sure. It was stupid not to report what I knew about the car, and even more stupid to go back to it. Fortunately, the surprisingly personable constable didn't seem to suspect me of anything, except being an idiot.

Constable Cropper, or apparently Colin to his friends, rose from the table, the chair scraping on the linoleum floor. 'And remember: no snooping around investigating. Miss Castle may have kept a spare key under the urn by the back door, but that doesn't mean it's there for you to use. Understood?'

He carefully donned his peaked cap and ensured it was straight. I blinked up at him, trying to assimilate what he had just said. A key hidden under… 'Aye,' I said. 'Message received and I think understood.'

Debbie and I stood to shake his hand before he left.

Once he was gone, she turned to me. 'Did what I think just happened, just happen?'

'PC Cropper warned us not to investigate Veronica's death on our own.'

'No, he just told us where the house key is kept. He wants us to go in there. And you know what that means, don't you?'

'Actually, I do,' I said with a nod and a wry smile. 'He also thinks something smells fishy about this, but he cannae investigate it himself. He needs our help. Come on, we've got to get you and the bairns home for your trip to the park.'

'Oh that can wait. We need to have a poke around Veronica's house.'

'We can't do that today or tomorrow. It's the weekend and there'll be umpteen tourists going down to the stones making nuisances of themselves.'

The path to Chalkdown Long Barrow went right past Frisky Pigeons, and the risk of being seen was too great. We may have had tacit police approval, but I was fairly sure that this would not be a great argument in court.

'Okay, Monday then,' Debbie agreed reluctantly. 'But you're right; we'd better go. Don't want to be late or we may not wear Satan's demons out before tonight.'

Seven

We arrived back in Downscliffe carrying the extra ballast of three hyperactive ten-year-olds on the back seat. They did not seem to have lost any energy since we had dropped them off three hours earlier. If anything, they had wound each other up even further. It was so good to see that Fergus had been accepted by his two new friends without question. The school was a microcosm of life in the village itself, and children there were just as resistant to newcomers as their parents and grandparents. Fergus had the added pressure of being one of the only ginger-haired kids in the school, and also speaking with a broad Aberdonian accent. Freddie and Arthur hadn't cared about any of this, though. They would argue furiously about which was the scarier enemy: the Cybermen or the Sontarans, but accent and physical appearance were irrelevant to them.

When we got to Debbie's house, it was still an enormous relief to eject the twins from the car. I didn't envy her the afternoon to come. Tony was outside, head buried under the stubby bonnet of his van. It was a mostly white Ford Transit, a little rough around the edges with rust stains around the wheel arches. He looked up when he heard Ernie's engine, and gave a lopsided smile from beneath a bushy moustache. I think he was going for the roguish Burt Reynolds look, but had ended up more like a confused Freddie Mercury.

'Right, that's us,' Debbie shouted at the boys in the back. 'You ready to terrorise the people at Knole Park?'

'Yay!' came two overenthusiastic responses. Ernie was just a two-door model, so she had to get out first to let the boys come bundling out from the back and go racing over to see their dad.

Tony had always struck me as one of those solid, dependable, and eminently accommodating men who lived for his family, and would always shift heaven and Earth to help his friends. He wasn't especially good looking (even without the Freddie Mercury 'tache), or tall or muscular, and didn't strike me as all that intelligent, but he had always treated Debbie well, and that was more than good enough for me.

The twins charged over to their father like a two-boy Viking horde. He managed to extricate himself from under the bonnet just in time to get rugby tackled, holding his oil-coated hands aloft. Debbie wouldn't thank him for getting thick, black sludge on the boys' clothes.

'Hi love,' he shouted over to Debbie.

'Wouldn't the van start?' she yelled back.

'Van's fine. It's called maintenance,' he protested, retrieving his pipe from his back pocket and relighting it, his head immediately engulfed in a cloud of sweet-smelling smoke.

'Yeah, right.' She turned back to me, flicking her eyes upward and shaking her head. 'Honestly, he's hopeless.'

'Of course he's hopeless; he's a man, isn't he?' I said, then poked my head around the side of her. 'Hey Tony, what's the buzz?'

'Morning Ginger,' he yelled back as he was buffeted by the small human whirlwinds. That had been his pet name for me, ever since we had danced at the Christmas do in the village hall the previous December. I really can't say that I was terribly bothered by the moniker. I've been called a lot worse.

'I'll call you tomorrow,' Debbie said. 'Let you know how tonight goes.' She raised her voice so half the lane could hear. 'That is, if Beelzebub's demonic ghoulies give us a moment's peace!'

The outburst did little to quell the boys' excitement, and after a couple of seconds of respite, they began again, tearing around and yelling like banshees.

Debbie slammed the door and stomped up the driveway. I had the distinct impression she would have much rather spent a quiet afternoon with me than with her two beloved children.

I pulled away, and saw Fergus waving frantically at his two friends. 'Fergs, I've just got to pop to the shop in the village. You coming along, or you want me to drop you home?'

We got to my driveway and stopped while Fergus considered the two options. He was not, with the best will in the world, one of life's most decisive people.

'Umm… I'll come with you.'

'As long as you're sure. I mean you haven't got a hot date with a groovy chick, have you?'

He screwed his face up. At the moment, girls were there to be endured. He had yet to discover that they could be useful for other things.

Instead of turning around in my driveway, I decided to take a slight detour further up the road. It was best to drive slowly along Ashfield Lane anyway, as kids had this alarming habit of emerging suddenly from driveways, either running or on bikes, but it suited me today as I had a chance to quickly study Veronica's house as I trundled past at little more than walking pace.

There was what looked like a converted coach in the driveway, in white and two-tone blue. I recognised the logo on the side as belonging to Southern TV. If I'd had my wits about me I might have noticed the word "Southern" printed in huge navy-blue letters on the slab sides of the vehicle. There were also half a dozen people milling about, peering around the truck. They kept close to the road, as if nervous about straying too close to the house. A man in a dark suit paced up and down, staring intently at a clipboard, while a cameraman and sound engineer leant against the outside broadcast bus. They looked significantly scruffier, with long, bushy hair, dirty t-shirts and flared trousers that might constitute a risk in high winds. I saw one of them take a last drag on his cigarette, before stubbing it out on the dead woman's driveway. In the few seconds it took to drive ponderously past the scene, I recognised some of the onlookers as women who I generally saw waiting at the school gates.

But no police were at the house, I noted. That would probably annoy the television crew. They liked to have police around; it made the scene appear more important.

'Is that her hoose, Mum?' Fergus asked. 'The wifey who died?'

'If you mean the lady who's tragically passed away, then yes.'

He shrugged off the correction. You could take the kid out of Aberdeen, but you couldn't take the Aberdeen out of the kid. 'They're saying her neck was stretched a foot long.' He held his hands about eighteen inches apart, indicating his approximation of how wide a foot was.

'I very much doubt that. Who's saying that anyway?'

'Freddie and Arthur. And their grandma.'

'Ferg, you know better than to trust what those two loons say, and as for their grandma, she should know better. Everything's just hearsay at the moment.'

At the top of the road was the Beverly Hillbillies' homestead – or the Willes' property, as it was more correctly known. They were a rough family, buying and selling whatever junk came their way, with not a great deal of concern over its provenance. The garden was a jungle, with a dozen or more rusting car bodies piled into a corner with grass taller than me growing through the slowly decaying chassis. The youngest son was a year older than Fergus, and had been caught with some of his mates bullying my boy several months before. The headmaster in the school was made abundantly clear of my feelings on this issue, and this six-foot man mountain was left jabbering after I had finished with him, and the issue of who was bullying whom became a little blurred for a while. However, the Willes boy's gang never bothered Fergus again.

Even so, I caught him looking warily at the house as we passed, but he soon relaxed once we had moved on.

I was not about to go back past Veronica's house, lest I be accused of the same rubbernecking ghoulishness as the women who stood at the end of the drive, so set off along the Pilgrims' Way. This stretch of the ancient Roman road hugged the foot of the Downs, a long, winding, perilously narrow metalled track that seemed to go on forever. In fact, it was the only road I had ever come across that seemed longer to drive than to walk. The turns and dips and blind crests came with nerve-jangling regularity. There were passing places, but more than one car had gone rolling down the twenty-foot embankment before, and I really did not wish to add to that number. I was extremely glad when we emerged from the far end and headed south along Downs Road.

I had a few bits and pieces to get from the shop, and a couple more things to learn about Veronica Castle.

Eight

The village grocery store and post office nestled just between the two pubs in the village, The Old Badger and The Blue Bell. It struck me as amusing, and an indication of the local population's priorities, that Downscliffe had one little village shop, and two pubs.

I pulled up outside the shop, parking two wheels on the pavement. Considering it was the main artery through the village, Downs Road was ridiculously narrow, bushy hedgerows creeping further and further into the lane on either side.

Fergus jumped out and was round to the drivers' side before I even had my door closed, still full of energy, while I made sure my sunglasses were firmly in place.

'Catriona!' a man's voice yelled from up the road.

I spun around to see who it was. Striding down the pavement, just passing the duck pond outside the entrance to Wimble's Farm was the rotund form of Derek Tucker,

77

the landlord of The Old Badger. He was lucky there was a slight downward incline, or I would fear he might collapse. He wore a cream heavy cotton shirt, over which he had an olive green gilet, which had become his favoured attire over the winter. I had the feeling that the waistcoat served less of a fashion purpose, but rather it helped keep his expanding belly in check.

'Fit like the day, Derek,' I shouted. He wasn't far away now but his hearing wasn't what it once was, and he did love it when I came out with the odd Doric expression.

'I'm glad I caught you,' he beamed. 'In fact, I've just been up to your place. I dropped a note in your door, but it's better I ask you in person. Your bread pudding is selling like you wouldn't believe. We've completely run out. I was wondering – well, hoping really – you might be able to knock up another batch this afternoon. Two if you could.' He pulled a handkerchief from his pocket and wiped some sweat from his face as he wheezed heavily.

I was a little taken aback. The bread pudding had been popular through the winter months, but once the weather had started to warm up, sales had naturally trailed off to a trickle. 'Aye, I'll start a double batch as soon as I get in. It's a bit unexpected, isn't it?'

He looked a little shifty, as he sought the right words. 'Umm… I take it you never saw the special edition of the Mercury this morning?'

I shook my head dumbly.

'There's a big feature on Veronica Castle. Front page stuff. And they've reprinted her review of The Old

Badger. At least, part of it. The part about your bread pudding.'

I closed my eyes and sighed. Just when I thought that unpleasant chapter of my life was over, it emerges again like an unwelcome smell from a drain that never goes away completely. 'Including the line that went, "a stodgy mess of confectionery excess"?'

'I'm afraid so, and went on to say, "like a Lucozade drizzle cake that floated limply in a lake of insipid custard".

'Aye, thanks for reminding me,' I grumbled.

'I still think that was grossly unfair,' he said, clapping a big, meaty arm around my shoulders. 'But the restaurant was *heaving* this lunchtime. Absolutely heaving, all of them wanting a piece of your bread pudding. And we're suddenly fully booked tonight. It's mad. The article has stirred up a lot of interest.'

'So it seems. Okay, I'll have two batches to you by seven o' clock.'

'Can you make it six? We're opening the restaurant an hour early tonight because of the rush.'

'Ugh. I'll see what I can do.' I felt a small hand tugging at my skirt, and looked down. The little freckled face that looked up at me was etched with concern.

'Mum, you said you'd do my costume,' Fergus pleaded.

'We can do that tonight, sweetheart,' I said, feeling a wave of guilt sweep over me. I hated having to let him down, on anything, but business had to come first. Or at least money. Without that, we'd be in real trouble.

'Promise?'

'Promise,' I smiled, and looked back to Derek. 'You see the heartbreak your corporate greed is causing, you great brute?'

He smiled back and ruffled Fergus's hair. 'My apologies, young sir. So, what about this Veronica business then, eh? Didn't see that one coming. Did you?'

'I don't think anyone did,' I replied, and knew it would be best to keep my suspicions to myself.

'Maybe she read some of her own articles and that sent her over the edge,' he quipped. 'Actually, I think perhaps it was one dalliance too many.'

It took a moment for that sentence to sink in. 'Dalliance? You mean she had a bit of a reputation?' I was well aware of her reputation, of course. It had been the subject of much discussion outside the school gates the previous afternoon.

'Well, I don't know. You hear things in the pub. Tongues loosen after a few drinks. People are wondering whether she got knocked back by one of her beaus, and that was why she did it.'

'Or maybe…' I began, but stopped myself. Maybe someone else was responsible, but for similar reasons. That was what I wanted to say, but kept my counsel. This wasn't the time.

'Yes?' he prompted with a lopsided frown.

'Oh, nothing. I was just thinking out loud. I need to get the ingredients for this bread pudding, so I'd better get going, Derek.'

'Of course,' he smiled, and looked down at a bored and disinterested Fergus. 'You look after your mum, young man.'

'Yes sir,' he replied with a stern resolve.

Derek went strolling back up toward The Old Badger, waving extravagantly to Stephen Wimble, assistant manager at the farm, as he went.

With a sigh, I pushed open the door to the shop, popping my sunglasses into my handbag. It stuck a little, and rattled heavily, the sound accompanied by the tinkling jangle of a bell. The shop was not quite ancient, especially when one considered the age of some buildings in the village, but from the oak beams and uneven walls, I wouldn't have said it was less than four hundred years old. It was a proper little food emporium, with more than the usual everyday essentials, but also produce from local bespoke suppliers.

At the sound of the bell, a woman came bustling back into the shop from the storeroom behind the counter. She wore a pale blue dress with a tabard just a shade darker, and a frilly white apron over the top. Her hair had been permed to within an inch of its life, curled ferociously like grey and blond springs, made even wilder by the Alice band that kept the fringe away from her eyes.

'Hello Maureen,' I said as the door clattered shut behind me.

She cocked her head to one side, peering over her reading glasses. 'Oh, hello Catriona, dear. I know why you're here.'

'You do?'

'Yes, Derek from the pub was just in here not half an hour ago. You'll be needing ingredients for a bread pudding. Am I right?'

'You're a mind reader, Maureen,' I grinned. 'I just found out myself. Now I have to try and remember what I've got. I know I need wholemeal bread. Have you got any on or near its sell-by date?'

'There's some out the back that went past yesterday. Would that be okay?'

'Perfect. I also need muscovado sugar; I know that. Oh, and a lemon.'

'No lemons, I'm afraid, dear.'

'Then we'll have to slum it with a squeezy of Jif. Oh, nearly forgot. Rich Tea biscuits and digestives.'

'For a bread pudding, my dear?' she asked, taking half a step back as if she'd just learned I had measles.

'No, I've been roped into entering the cake making contest for jubilee day. I need to get some practice in.'

'Right you are, dear. As a matter of fact, I was hoping to run into you.'

'Oh really? Why?'

'Well, I suppose you've heard about… You know… The unfortunate occurrence on Ashfield Lane.'

'Ah, you mean Veronica Castle's suicide.'

Maureen closed her eyes, putting a fluttering hand to her chest as she whispered a silent prayer. 'But it does leave the Jubilee Celebration Committee in a bit of a quandary. You see, Veronica was supposed to be our judge.'

'I know. I had wondered about that. Without her, I'm not sure the contest can go ahead, with no one to judge it, if you see what I mean.'

'Well that's just the point, you see,' Maureen said as she totted up the cost of everything. Shopping in the Downscliffe village shop was probably slightly more expensive than shopping at Fortnum & Mason or Harrods. 'I was talking to the other members of the committee last night, and we all thought – well, wondered – if you would consider being our judge? There really is no one else. I mean, no one of your calibre, of course.'

I wanted to tell her just how thrilled I was at being the committee's last resort, but I refrained. She was clearly suffering enough and frankly, I didn't have the heart to torture the poor woman unduly. 'I would be honoured, Maureen. I'll still take the cake ingredients, though. I'll be needing to get into practice.'

'Oh, that's such a relief!' she seemed to deflate like a rapidly emptying balloon, and for a worrying instant, I thought she might collapse altogether. 'I can't tell you how frantic the other members and me have been since we heard the news. You know, the news of—'

'I can imagine. Is there anything in particular that I need to do?'

'No, no, just make sure you can be at the baking marquee by two-fifteen on Monday. The day of the jubilee celebration?'

'Of course.' *Really? That Monday? Why not Monday in six weeks' time?* 'I'll be there anyway. Fergus will be entering the fancy dress contest at two, and we won't want to miss the floats that go by at eleven.' I clutched him to me, his shoulder hitting my hip with a significant thump.

'Wonderful. Between you and me,' she said, lowering her voice to a conspiratorial level and leaning toward me, 'I was never keen on having that Veronica as our judge. One does hate to speak ill of the dead...'

But that's not going to stop you, I thought.

'...but she did have something of a reputation, and there was a danger that she might engulf the Downscliffe Jubilee Committee in scandal.'

'Really? What kind of scandal?'

'Well...' Maureen was flustered again; possibly even more than when asking me to be the baking contest last-minute replacement judge. She quickly removed her glasses and began to clean the lenses on her apron. 'Can I trust you to keep a secret?'

'Certainly. I can be the very model of discretion.' *When I want to be.*

'As I understand it, and I have it on good authority, but Veronica was involved with... I could hardly believe it myself.'

'Go on,' I urged, trying not to sound too impatient. *Just get on with it, woman.*

'She was involved in what can only be described as an illicit affair with someone from the village. From this village, I ask you?'

'No! How shocking. You kind of wonder where she found the energy,' I mumbled, and earned myself a frown of rebuke from the shopkeeper. Apparently flippant remarks were not acceptable when discussing the rampant promiscuity of the recently deceased. 'I don't suppose you have any idea who this gentleman might have been?'

'It's really not for me to say, dear. But this reputation of hers wasn't just a recent thing, either. I know who she really was.'

'Well… we do know who she was. Don't we?'

She shook her head, revelling in her little secret. I was positively itching to find out myself, and was almost ready to drag the information out of her by any means I could muster, possibly involving thumbscrews and sodium pentothal.

'We all know who she wanted us to think she was, but not who she had been thirty year ago.' She lowered her voice to a whisper. 'You see, dear, most people think she just moved to the village two year ago, but that ain't the whole truth. Her family was originally *from* this village. I actually went to school with her, back at the tail end of the war, but the family moved away in '48. There was a scandal.'

'Involving Veronica?'

She nodded. 'Involving Veronica. Of course, that wasn't her name back then. There were rumours of an affair. Someone quite well respected in the village, as I understand it. And… a pregnancy.'

A Three Villages Mystery

'Veronica was pregnant?' I gasped, and realised my mouth was open in astonishment, hand over my chest. 'I never knew she had any kids.'

'To be honest with you, dear, I don't know what happened to the child. Or what happened to Veronica until she turned up in the village a couple a year ago. I couldn't believe it when she came walking into my shop, bold as brass, after nigh on three decades. Most people didn't recognise her. She wasn't blond back then. No, she had the most gorgeous dark brown hair. And such a pretty thing, she was. But a mouthy little madam as well.'

'She clearly didn't change *that* much then. So, what was her name back then?'

There was another tinkle from the bell as someone else entered, accompanied by the clatter of the ill-fitting door. This seemed to be enough to distract Maureen from her train of thought and the moment was gone.

'How do?' Burt Stickels asked, touching finger and thumb to his flat cap in a peculiar, almost naval salute. His donkey jacket had an ever present aroma of old pipe tobacco – not unpleasant, but I wouldn't want to get stuck in a lift with him for too long. It was rare to see Bert out and about like this. Almost invariably, I only ever saw him on his push bike, freewheeling along Downs Road to the Old Badger, pushing the bike back up again, or keeping the bar staff company in the pub.

'Afternoon Bert,' Maureen said, a touch louder than normal. Bert was known to be quite deaf. When he wanted to be.

A Jubilee Murder

I quickly handed over a five pound note to Maureen and gathered up the two bags of shopping. There was the familiar ching-ching as she rang it up on the till, and the cash drawer sprung out. Thankfully, five pounds was enough and Fergus collected the change for me. I thanked her for emptying my bank account and said my goodbyes as I lurched unsteadily out of the shop, Fergus trying not to get run over in the process.

That was enough Nancy Drewing for one day. I had two trays of bread pudding to make.

Nine

hen we got home, Fergus scurried off to his room to play until it was time to settle down in front of the television. It was Saturday night with no Doctor Who and no Space 1999, but there was The Muppet Show, which he wasn't about to miss just because I had to deliver a couple of bread puddings.

I quickly changed out of the prim skirt, blouse, waistcoat and boots ensemble and threw on some faded old jeans that I had probably bought in the late sixties, and light sweater. As ancient as the outfit might be, it was much more suited to some messy baking.

This was a job for Mr Bucket. Perhaps I should clarify that Mr Bucket was my biggest mixing bowl. It was a whopper, but I needed a whopper if I was going to knock up a double batch of bread pudding in under three hours. Time was short. I had spent too long trying to coax details out of Maureen, only for Bert to come blundering in and ruin the moment. Talk about a total gooseberry.

There was one upside to the situation, though.

A Jubilee Murder

Bread pudding is a great way to work off frustrations. All that tearing of bread and scrunching the gooey mixture together was quite cathartic, and it also helped to clear the mind and allow me to focus. Rip, squeeze, squelch, scrunch. A few minutes of that and seeing sultanas and mixed peel oozing between my fingers was enough to help my conscious mind drift off over the horizon.

Veronica Castle. My mind kept coming back to her, the name floating off to the periphery, before returning to the fore. It seemed she had a history. Maureen was infamous as being one of the worst gossips in the village, and much of what she said I normally took with a hefty sack of salt. But there was something about the way she had spoken that had given the story some credibility.

I tried to get things straight in my own head. Veronica (or whatever her name had been back then) had gotten herself involved in an affair with a married man in Downscliffe. No, I corrected myself. He may not have been married, but he was a prominent figure in the village, and the scandal had been notorious enough to force Veronica and her family to leave. It appeared that a pregnancy had forced the issue. What had happened to the child? Had she had an abortion? Maybe, but it would have been unusual and still quite dangerous back in the late forties, not to mention illegal. It wasn't until '68 that the law had been changed to allow abortions. I discounted the pregnancy for now. There was too little to go on to factor it in. So, this teenage girl had left the village, changed her name and gone off to make her fortune.

A Three Villages Mystery

So, it begged the question: why would she come back? It may have been three decades, but there were still those in the village who would remember her, like Maureen Bishop in the shop. Would someone *kill* her to keep the story from resurfacing? It sounded unlikely, but people had killed for less. Who was this notable individual, whose eye turned toward a pretty teenage girl way back in 1948? His identity might be the key to the whole thing.

I realised I'd been ripping and squelching for ten full minutes, and the mixture was as well worked as any I had ever made. Thankfully, this was quite a forgiving recipe, so no harm had been done. I tried to keep a little more focused as I mixed in the eggs and muscovado sugar.

I dearly wanted to get inside Veronica's house and have a poke about. It was clear that the police had not suspected foul play when they visited the house on Friday. And why would they? It looked clear-cut enough. There was no sign of a struggle; no violence; no marks to the body that suggested anything other than a suicide. In fact, that was a puzzle. If someone was trying to hang her, wouldn't she have fought back at all?

I hoped there might be some clues in her house as to the identity of this mystery man. I couldn't think of anyone who might fit the bill. I thought initially of the school headmaster, but swiftly discounted him. He had not been in the village much longer than I had. Derek Tucker had taken over the lease in The Old Badger around fifteen years before, although I didn't know whether he had connections to Downscliffe before that. It was a similar story for the landlord of The Blue Bell. The vicar had…

The vicar. He was not an in-aboot comer like the rest. He had been the pastor to the village for many years. Had he been around thirty years before? I wasn't sure, but one thing I did know was that he knew a lot of this village's secrets. He was Anglican, so there was no formal confessional as such, but people told a clergyman things that they didn't tell other people. Except perhaps their barkeeper. I could speak to Derek again when I dropped off the bread puddings. I was fairly sure that I could persuade him to elaborate on what we had spoken about earlier.

My shoulders and head sagged. In fact, my whole body sagged and it would have looked to anybody watching that I was about to collapse into the gooey bread mix. Veronica's last stop before heading home, apparently to hang herself, had been the church. There was no getting away from it; I would have to speak to the creepy old vicar. I didn't want to leave this until Monday, so would attend the Sunday service in the morning. Hopefully, I could catch him either before or after the service.

I glanced up at the clock that ticked away on the wall, like a metronomic musical accompaniment to my baking. Four o' clock. If I didn't get a move on, Derek wouldn't have any bread pudding to feed his guests with.

The mixture was ready, so I poured it into a pair of baking trays and patted the top with my palm, teasing the surface to a rough finish. After giving them a generous dusting of demerara, I popped them into the oven. Over the next hour and a half, I swapped them around a couple of times so they would cook more evenly.

At a quarter to six, I brushed myself off. I was generally a messy baker, and a day rarely went by where I wasn't liberally coated in flour, or left picking sultanas out of my hair. I told Fergus that I was off out. We had made a deal: he could stay home tonight and watch The Muppet Show, as long as he came with me to church in the morning. With a sigh and a lop-sided frown that made him look like he was having a stroke, he agreed to the bargain. Church tomorrow was marginally better than missing Kermit, Fozzie, Miss Piggy and Gonzo et al tonight.

Ten

Within ten minutes of them coming out of the oven, I had loaded two trays of bread pudding into the back of Ernie and headed off down to the village. It was approaching six p.m., and the sun was low enough in the sky to be obscured by the treetops, flickering intermittently as I drove down the hill.

They had been busy in the village during the afternoon. Bunting was in the process of being strung from every lamppost and from every gutter. I saw a tractor with a large bucket attachment at the front roaring along Downs Road. In the bucket were three extremely eager and I suspected extremely drunk "helpers", fixing bunting and EIIR posters to any available surface. I wondered which would come first: the job being completed, or one of the helpers falling out of the bucket and breaking his neck.

When I got to The Old Badger, the car park was already half full. It seemed that Derek hadn't been exaggerating and that Veronica's death had really been a boost to his business. Despite the fact that I had disliked her with a passion, there seemed to be something mildly distasteful about profiting from her untimely demise. Still, that was a matter for his conscience, and considering he had been hurt by Veronica's review just as much as I had, I didn't think he was expending too much effort wrestling with his conscience. As one of his suppliers, neither was I.

The Old Badger was the locals' pub, the place where you would find old men nursing pints of warm bitter, where farm hands and tractor drivers escaped to at lunchtimes to grab a sandwich and a pint, before heading back to the yard. The lower floor was bare red brick on the outside, the colours muted by age. Above these, the upper level was clad in worn old wood panelling, painted white an indeterminate number of years/decades earlier, peeling away at the edges. The Blue Bell, a hundred and fifty yards along Downs Road, was a more tourist friendly place and catered to families with a kids' play area in the beer garden. Derek had steadfastly refused to countenance any such modernisation. This was a locals' pub, and as long as his name was above the door, that was the way it would remain, thank you very much.

I had already decided against going through the public or lounge bars of the pub brandishing two trays of steaming bread pudding. The last thing I wanted was to be accosted by journalists or plain old ghoul hunters, who would attempt to prize out every last morsel of gossip about the deceased celebrity that they could. They might as well have left her carcass out on display for the vultures to pick at.

I went around the back to the kitchen entrance where I knew Dotty, the cook, would be. The exterior paintwork around the windows and door here was in an even sorrier state, coming away in large, curly strips. The wood beneath was grey and cracked now that it was exposed to the elements. Dirty cobwebs shrouded the windows and hung like gossamer veils from cracked gutters. One day, perhaps sooner rather than later, Derek would have to reach into his bulging wallet and pull out a few shillings for a spot of redecorating.

The kitchen door was ajar, its glass panes coated in an impenetrable layer of condensation. On the stove, multiple saucepans had steam pouring from them, lids sitting at jaunty angles and rattling away. There were two people in the kitchen: Dotty, the eternally grumpy and flush-faced cook who was always threatening to chuck her grubby apron on the floor and storm out, and her equally unenthusiastic assistant, Gemma.

'Dotty?' I shouted through the steam. It was around this time that I realised just how heavy two large trays of bread pudding could be, as I balanced them on the palm of one hand, one of my tea towels protecting my fingertips. Bread pudding retained its heat for a long time. At some point, I was sure that a NASA scientist would realise that bread pudding would be the perfect insulation in winter and all homes would be made from it.

At the sound of my voice, the plump woman looked

round. She didn't exactly look pleased to see me, more relieved. The Old Badger's kitchen was not normally this busy, and she was clearly a very stressed woman. 'Oh, at last. I thought you weren't coming.'

'Wouldnae miss it for the world,' I replied with a smile. I could afford to be upbeat. I wasn't the one slaving away in a scorching hot kitchen. 'Where do you want these bread puddings, Dotty?' I asked, looking around for an empty surface, but finding none. It turned out, Dotty was just as disorganised in the kitchen as I was. She bustled over and took them from me, turning in a full circle twice as she too sought somewhere to dump them.

'Gemma, here, find somewhere to put these,' she said, plonking the two trays in the girl's arms, who went wobbling off into the annex to deposit them. 'Ugh, it's a ruddy madhouse around here right now. Never known it so busy. His nibs says it's all your fault with that article, but I dunno. All I do know is he don't pay me enough for all this. Not by a long chalk.'

I wasn't quite sure what a "long chalk" was, but I got the general idea. 'I'm sure it's only temporary. Veronica was famous. Well, sort of famous. I mean we're not talking Larry Grayson or Bruce Forsyth kind of famous here. Mostly just famous in the Southern TV region. But in a few days I'm sure all the interest will have died down.'

'I ruddy well hope—' The jangling of a timer alarm interrupted her and she sneered, pulling a face uncannily similar to the one Fergus demonstrated when I told him we were going to church in the morning. She waddled over to the cooker and lifted a pan, slamming it down on the draining board, boiling water sloshing over the edge and onto the floor.

'I ought to go and find Derek,' I said, eager to leave her to it. I liked to think of myself as healthily disorganised. This place was sheer bedlam, and I could hardly wait to escape. 'Is he in the bar?'

'More likely he's in the restaurant, schmoozing the punters.'

'Aye, good luck,' I said, smiling again.

Dotty didn't reciprocate, merely sneering with glum resignation.

The transition from kitchen to bar restaurant could not have been starker. In a second, I had moved from a broiling chaos to a good humoured, genteel environment where customers politely laughed and chatted. It must have been reasonably warm in the restaurant, but compared to the kitchen it was positively, blissfully chilly. There was the obligatory red, white and blue bunting hanging from the oak beams, and the EIIR royal cypher was on the wall to the side of the bar, "tastefully" fashioned with beer mats and balloons.

There were two waitresses working tonight. I didn't know the younger one, a girl with shoulder length hair unbelievably even more ginger than my own, her face suffering the same blotchy redness as mine was prone to. The other I did know. Her name was Marianne, and she represented everything I wasn't: dark-haired with a flawless complexion, tall, slim, elegant and effortlessly beautiful. It would be so easy to hate someone like that, but I didn't. No one did. The most annoying thing of all was that she was utterly lovely, kind and caring with not a hint of malice.

'Evening Marianne, how's the course going?' I asked as she finished delivering a trolley of prawn cocktails and cream of tomato soups to a table, giving her a self-conscious little wave. I recalled her telling me that she was doing a botany degree at the agricultural research college in Swanhurst East. Science would be a career, she had told me; waitressing paid the bills.

'Hello Catriona,' she greeted me in the hushed tones of a good waitress. 'Going well, thanks. Way too much to learn and I've got exams coming up, so I'm terrified of those. But other than that, all's good. Are you looking for Derek? I think he's around here somewhere.' She cast about, looking for her boss.

'Ah, I see him,' I said, spotting the landlord at the bar talking to a pair of what looked like farm workers. I felt a knot suddenly form in the pit of my gut as I realised who these men were: Barry Huckstep, the creepy tractor driver, and Terry Willes, the hillbilly from the top of Ashfield Lane. Barry filled me with a morbid dread after our encounter at the church. Terry filled me with rage as I thought of how his feral, vindictive son had bullied Fergus.

It was at that moment that a thought struck me, and I couldn't believe how stupid I'd been not to see it before.

Terry Willes. I didn't have the scrap of paper on me, but I remembered what it said well enough: T. Wills. That was a little too close to be discounted. But what possible connection could he have with Veronica?

'Catriona!' Derek bellowed across the room, and patted Terry on the shoulder before striding over to me.

I had almost been in a daze, and actually shook my head to cast away the cobwebs. For a moment, I made eye contact with Barry Huckstep, but there was no acknowledgement in his face, no nod of greeting or hint of a smile. He immediately went back to talking in hushed tones to Terry.

Derek held out his hands like Pat Jennings, preparing to face a penalty kick. 'Did you get them done?'

'Aye, they're done. Dotty has them.'

'Oh, marvellous!' he shouted. 'Ladies and gentlemen, for those that are thinking about pudding, our saviour has arrived. This amazing young lady has brought a fresh batch of her wonderful bread puddings, loved by everyone who tries them. Well, almost everyone.'

There was a ripple of subdued chuckles from those who had read Veronica's delightful review. It seemed that the majority of diners this evening were familiar with it, which I was less than thrilled about.

Derek put his arm around Marianne's waist and clutched her tightly to him. 'Marianne, I think table four is ready to order.'

'Yes, Mr Tucker,' she replied, awkwardly extricating herself from his grasp. She smoothed her apron and flicked away a stray lock of hair before weaving her way through the crowded restaurant to take the order.

'Wonderful girl,' he said, his eyes locked on her receding form until he could see her no more. 'Now, I think it's time for your reward, don't you?'

'If you've got time,' I said. I felt for poor Marianne. Derek had a bit of a reputation in the village. Dirty Derek, most of the girls called him, his wandering hands infamous among waiting and bar staff who were always young and female. Mercifully, a ginger-haired thirty-three-year-old Scottish woman with too many freckles and blotchy skin in the hot weather fell outside his field of interest.

I squeezed past Bert, who was sat at the bar, probing away at the last charred remains of tobacco in his pipe and tapping it out into an ashtray. 'How do,' he mumbled as I pressed myself against the bar, trying to take up as little space as possible and easing my backside onto a stool. Derek lifted the hatch and joined the barmaid. I noticed again how tactile he was with the young women, although tactile might have been an overly generous term. Eventually, I was sure, this wishful philandering was going to get him into trouble.

'Now, two bread pudding trays,' he said when he reached the till. 'What's that, eight pounds?'

'Twelve,' I corrected him.

'Are you sure it wasn't ten?'

'It's still twelve, Derek.'

A Jubilee Murder

'Twelve pounds,' Bert echoed, shaking his head sorrowfully. 'Twelve pounds for a bread pudding.' He harrumphed, and I couldn't tell whether he thought this was an outstanding bargain, or astonishingly overpriced.

'Twelve pounds sounds like an awful lot to me,' Derek persisted. 'You're absolutely sure you won't take ten?'

'Let me think a moment…' I said, tapping a finger repeatedly against my lips. 'Hmm… no. I think I'll still take twelve if it's all the same to you. Unless you want me to retrieve them from Dotty and I'll see if The Blue Bell want them?'

'No, no, that's all right,' Derek said, holding up a hand. He knew this was just the game we always played. He knew it; I knew it; everyone in the village knew it. It was well known in the parish that he had what was generally excused as "wandering hands", but he was also notorious for being the biggest tightwad this side of the English Channel. He opened the till, the machine making a ferocious jangling rattle, and withdrew a tenner and two one-pound notes. It seemed to cause him almost physical pain to part with them.

'Ah, thank you, kind sir,' I said, and immediately compounded his agony. 'Did you say you were going to buy me a drink as well?'

'No, I don't think—'

'I mean, it really *was* very short notice, and I really did get you out of a wee bit of bother, didn't I?'

'Well it was good of you, I admit, but—'

'Och, you are kind. I'll have a glass of dry white wine. Make sure it's properly chilled, would you, sweetie?'

He knew when he was beaten, and capitulated without further protest. For a ghastly moment I thought he was going for the Blue Nun, but thankfully his hand slipped past it and he withdrew half a bottle of Chablis from the fridge. Not even the cheap house stuff. 'I'm glad you're on *my* side, Catriona,' he said, but there was no hint of peevishness, just an acknowledgement that he wouldn't always have it his own way.

'G'way ye go, min. Just imagine if I was your enemy,' I said, and then took a sip of wine. Oh, that was good. Crisp and fruity, but smooth as well. I leaned in closer. 'Derek,' I said with a slight gesticulation of my head.

'What is it?' he asked, holding a glass up to one of the optics and measuring himself a Glenfiddich. 'Finally ready to succumb to my advances?'

'No chance, you glaikit old reprobate,' I said with a wink. 'You know Veronica was going to be the judge of the baking competition on jubilee day?'

'Yes, and they've asked you to do it instead,' he said, tasting the whisky.

'How did you know?'

'There's not a lot that goes on in this village that I don't hear about. Several members of the Jubilee Committee drink in this pub.'

I was a little deflated to have my thunder stolen, but

carried on nonetheless. 'So I'm now judging the contest that Veronica was supposed to be. How's that for irony?'

'I'm sure she'd have been thrilled for you.'

'I'm sure it would've been *me* she'd strung up from the rafters. Derek, I was talking to Maureen in the shop earlier.'

'Oh yes? I bet she had a few choice things to say about our Veronica.'

'You're not wrong. Did you know that she used to live in the village way back?'

He paused for a moment, not answering immediately, swirling his whisky round in the glass. 'I had heard a rumour about that. Came back to her home village to die. There's a certain poetry to that, don't you think?'

'Maybe. I'm not a poet. Maureen said that there was some kind of scandal, and that it was so bad, Veronica's family had to leave. I was wondering who the alleged affair was with? I doubt it would matter now, since her family left almost thirty years ago, but I was curious.'

'Not all of them,' Derek said, and this certainly garnered my attention.

'Not all? You mean there's still someone here? In the village right now?'

'It's a difficult thing to cut off all ties with your home, Catriona, as I'm sure you know all too well.'

I nodded and took another sip of wine, the point well taken. When I said nothing more, he continued.

'This was all before my time in Downscliffe, so what I know is little more than hearsay, but as I understand it, there is a member of the family still in the village. Lives up your road, in fact. You know Wally Moore?

'Wally Moore? Wally Moore who found her body? He's a blood relative?'

'I know. What are the chances, eh? Old Wally Moore just happened to find his own niece's body hanging from the rafters.'

Wally's place was about halfway between Frisky Pigeons and Veronica's house. I hadn't given it a second thought at the time. He had said that he happened to be walking past and saw her door open. What if there were more to it than that?

'Wally's brother, Cuthbert, was her father. By all accounts, she was a real stunner back then. A pretty young girl, with a libido to match, so I hear.'

'Very pretty young lass,' Bert mumbled next to me.

It took a few seconds for what he had said to work its way through my thick skull and into my brain, like rainwater through a leaky ceiling. I turned to look at Bert. He sat there nodding slowly, and looking mournfully at his empty glass.

'Time I were off,' he grunted, and began to shift himself from the stool.

'Would you like another drink, Bert?' I asked, putting a hand on his forearm. He stopped and considered this.

'I'll miss Kojak if I stay too long,' he mumbled. 'But mebbe just a quick one.'

Derek grabbed the old man's glass and refilled it, heaving back on the pump a couple of times until the pint glass was once again full, a frothy head bubbling on top.

'You knew Veronica back then?' I asked, and took another sip of my wine. I would surely have appreciated another, but I was driving.

Bert harrumphed again, and took a sizable gulp of his bitter. 'I remember her. Of course, she were no called Veronica back then. She were just Bessie Moore. There weren't a male eye in the village that didn't turn when she went past. A real beauty, a real beauty.'

'I heard there was a pregnancy. Do you know what happened to the child?'

'Mr Tucker,' Marianne interrupted, appearing between Bert and me, 'the people at table three would like a word with you.'

'I'll be right over.' Derek finished his whisky in a single gulp and smacked his lips, savouring the flavour, before wandering over to talk to the diners.

'She got into trouble, all right,' Bert continued. 'But we never heard what happened to the young 'un. There were rumours, but that's all they were. Rumours. I don't think anyone really knew what had happened to it.'

'That's a pity. It would've been interesting to find out.'

'Except for Wally Moore, of course. He knew, but he's never let on. Not a word to no one.'

'That's fascinating. I wonder if he'd be a little more receptive to opening up now she's gone?'

A Three Villages Mystery

'I wouldn't count on it. Friendly as they come, Wally Moore is, but he's also a very private bloke. Not many who've ever gotten that close to him.' He took another hefty gulp of bitter, and set the empty glass down with a clunk. 'Now I really do 'ave to be going, young Catriona.'

'There's just one more thing, Bert. I still don't know. Who was it that Veronica – or rather, Bessie – had an affair with?'

'Oh, that's easy enough to answer. Jack Wimble, now the owner of Wimble's Farm. His father owned it at the time, and Jack was already married to Kitty. She weren't best pleased, I can tell you. Anyway, time for the off. Pleasure to talk to you, m'dear.'

'Thank you, Bert. Take care,' I smiled, and watched as the old man slowly weaved his way through the crowds, and started on his way home.

Home, a cup of tea and an hour of Kojak didn't sound too bad. Besides, I now had a gazillion thoughts tumbling round in my head, and needed to get the incoherent jumble in some sort of order.

Eleven

Fergus had hoped he'd get away with it, that somehow I might have forgotten our little bargain, but there was no chance of that. If I had to go to church, then he was going with me. What made it even worse for him, and what he had failed to consider, was that this was church, and at church he had to wear a suit. His argument that God didn't care what clothes you wore, as long as you're a good person may or may not have been accurate, but it didn't butter many parsnips with me. Like it or not, going to church in this village meant dressing the part, lest we incur the wrath of, if not God, then certainly Mrs Popplewell and her ilk.

There was more leeway afforded to the village's female parishioners, so I wore a three-quarter length dress with a muted floral pattern. Surely that would not offend the delicate sensibilities of the regulars. I just had to hope that a bare ankle did not incite a riot. Strangely, I was actually able to envisage the scene of a rampaging mob of irate parishioners trashing the place like a mob of skinheads, and leading the hussy responsible to the village green where she would be burned at the stake. I have quite a vivid imagination sometimes.

The service at St Luke's Church was due to kick off at… No, scratch that. Was due to *start* at ten-thirty. Best not liken it to a football match, lest I do anything else to annoy the congregation. I thought we scrubbed up quite well today. I hopefully wouldn't offend the Almighty with my brazen ankles. Fergus was trussed up like Little Lord Fauntleroy, and could not have looked more miserable about it.

It was such a gorgeous early summer's day that for a moment, I considered walking down to the church. But only for a moment, mind. Getting there was easy enough. Downhill all the way and after a rare couple of rainless days, if we took the direct route to the church across the field, there would be few muddy patches to negotiate. Apart from a bit at the far end of the footpath. For some reason, that little area never seemed to dry out completely. Getting back was another matter. It would mean traipsing up a significant hill with no shade in the heat of the midday sun. No, thank you very much. My alabaster Caledonian skin was not keen on the hot weather at the best of times, and this was inviting trouble.

We left at the stroke of eleven-and-a-bit minutes past ten. As we passed Debbie's house I slowed right down to peek in. There was no sign of life and the curtains were all still drawn. I was assuming that she'd had quite a late night, and I would have wagered that a fair quantity of alcohol would have been consumed. There was no sign of the twins either, and for a moment I wondered whether she had drugged them, or possibly tied them up and locked them in a cupboard. No, Debbie wouldn't really do that. Would she? I decided it was best not to pursue this line of thought and moved on.

I wanted to get to the church early, partly to secure one of the coveted parking spots, but also to catch any of the gossip that was bound to dominate proceedings. After all, I was sure that gossip was the main reason half of these people got up and went to church on a Sunday, and today there was only going to be one topic of conversation. Well, there may be a passing mention of the antics of the baked bean fiend who was still terrorising the neighbourhood, but apart from that, the only topic of interest was the death of our local celebrity. The police may have deemed it "just" a suicide, with no mysterious circumstances to suggest otherwise, but that wouldn't stop Veronica's death being the primary topic of conversation this weekend.

I parked Ernie in a prime position, just opposite the church, next to the low stone wall overlooking the cricket pitch. I could see that the pavilion was open and a couple of figures were moving around, making preparations for today's match. I'd seen a flyer pinned to the notice board in the village saying that Downscliffe would be playing Highview Village CC. Our village had lost against their local rivals from the top of the Downs on the previous three meetings, so this was something of a grudge match.

A Three Villages Mystery

There were already several cars at the church, and parishioners braver than I arriving on foot as well. The vicar was nowhere to be seen, and was presumably inside the church preparing for the service. As I opened the car door, the bells began to chime in a chirpily discordant manner. I heard them every weekend, and often wondered why they rang so close to the time of the service. I was sure that there was no way – absolutely no way – that I could ever hope to sling on some clothes, wrench a brush through the recalcitrant ball of string that was my hair, and drive down to the church in fifteen minutes. I had come to the conclusion that this was not a call to prayer, but merely a tradition that had endured over the centuries.

I was not a regular churchgoer, usually limiting my visits to Christmas and Easter, but from what I could see, all the usual faces were in attendance. There was Barbara Johnson, the leader of the coven who I knew from the school gates, along with a couple of her cohorts whom she had clearly harangued into attending. There were Jack and Kitty Wimble from the farm, and…

'It's unusual to see you here, isn't it dear?' came the haughty voice that I was never pleased to hear.

There was a tug at the side of my dress from Fergus, demanding my attention. I looked first to him, and then at Mrs Popplewell who had snuck up behind me. She must have snuck. That was what she did. I was sure the only way anyone would ever talk to her was if they were caught in an ambush.

'Oh, good morning, Mrs Popplewell,' I said, a smile

frozen on my face. 'It's a lovely day, don't you think?'

She harrumphed. 'They still haven't caught them, then,' she remarked. 'The village is gripped by a reign of terror and the police have done nothing.'

'But I thought… Have the police decided it *was* a murder, after all?'

'Murder? Catriona, my child, what on Earth are you talking about? Unless *I* catch them, of course. Then there may very well *be* a murder.'

I was completely nonplussed by the exchange and wanted to run away from the mad woman. Only the scant preservation of what remained of my dignity prevented me from doing so. And then the penny began to drop, almost like watching golden syrup drip slowly from a spoon, my addled brain latching onto a memory of the last time she and I had spoken.

'Oh, you mean the baked bean bandit. Still not caught him then, eh?'

She frowned at me, clearly disapproving of the term. As far as I was concerned, I was simply upholding a tradition of supplying catchy names to notorious criminals, like Jack the Ripper or Spring-heeled Jack. Come to think of it, why were so many Victorian villains called Jack? I cast a quick glance over to Jack Wimble, who was speaking to the Reverend Cackett. No, the farmer may be guilty of many things, but I doubted he crept around the village late at night throwing the contents of baked bean tins over cars and front doors.

'But why would you say murder, dear?' She

suddenly clapped a hand to her chest as she gasped. 'You mean poor Veronica was murdered?'

Will you haud yer weesht? I thought, silently cursing the biggest gob in Downscliffe, but kept the smile frozen on my face. 'Oh no, I didn't mean her. I'm not sure what I meant. Sorry, didn't mean to give you a heart attack.' I laughed nervously, hoping she would let the subject drop, or actually *have* a heart attack. I wasn't sure which eventuality would be more preferable at this point.

'Who's been murdered?' came another voice. Stephen Wimble appeared at my side. Jack and Kitty's son was in his mid-twenties, over six foot and almost strikingly handsome. I say almost because there was something about his face that hadn't been put together quite right. It wasn't as if they'd put his nose where his eyebrow should be, but there was just something very slightly off about him, like Simon MacCorkindale in one of those wobbly mirrors you get at the funfair.

'No one's been murdered,' I blurted, desperately trying to avoid saying "yet", as Mrs Popplewell's chances of surviving the day were rapidly diminishing. 'Merely a misunderstanding. Mrs Popplewell was just telling me that they still haven't caught the baked bean fiend yet.'

'Oh that,' he said, emitting a raucous bark of laughter.

'Honestly, young Mr Wimble,' Mrs Popplewell chided. 'This is a serious business, and I do not think the Sunday service is the correct place for such vulgar behaviour.'

He pulled a face at me, acknowledging that he had been well and truly ticked off for his outburst. It was all I could do not to burst out laughing as well. Unfortunately, there was one element that I had not factored in. Fergus cackled with laughter, burying his face in the folds of my dress.

Mrs Popplewell was certainly not amused.

What with Mrs Popplewell staring daggers at anyone within sight, and Fergus and wonky Simon MacCorkindale lowering the tone of proceedings, it was probably a good thing that us stragglers began to shuffle inside.

St Luke's had the feel of an ancient building inside as well as out. The walls were painted a stark white, the side windows narrow and tapering to a point. Even these smaller windows had surprisingly ornate stained glass images featuring the Virgin Mary, Christ and various prophets and apostles. At either end were enormous, three-paned stained glass windows, as large and ornate as anything that might be found in a church five times the size of St Luke's. For the edifice's relatively small size, the vaulted roof stretched high into the air, criss-crossed by wooden beams stained almost black by age. Directly opposite the entrance porch was a disproportionately large and exquisitely ornate pulpit, with a spiral staircase leading up to it. At the far end was the narthex, which Fergus thought was easily the most interesting aspect of this venerable place. In this small annex, tucked away from the nave where the congregation now began to take their seats, were several locked glass cabinets. In these were kept bones retrieved from Chalkdown Long Barrow, including a number of intact skulls. Fergus's ghoulish curiosity was no different to any other boy's, and when I was a teenager, I was no stranger to the macabre myself.

As soon as we were inside, he abandoned me and raced to the back of the church to make sure all the skeletal remains were still there, almost knocking over a couple of unsteady pensioners in the process. He plonked himself down on the very back row and beckoned for me to join him. As much as I would have liked to hide away at the back, I knew I ought to look a little more sociable. Maybe in twenty years, I would begin to be accepted as a bona fide villager, and then I could be as antisocial as I liked, but that was a long way off and we needed to look as if we were at least *trying* to integrate.

I pointed to Fergus, and then at a pew around halfway along the aisle. His shoulders sank. He knew that pointy finger. It was the pointy finger I used when I didn't want to be argued with. He and I were often not averse to a "lively debate", when he wanted his own way and I wouldn't let him, but this was not one of those times. He dragged himself from the bench and stomped down the aisle toward me, his grey woollen suit looking stiff and uncomfortable. I had the feeling it would take more than Kermit and Co. to get him to church again after this. Not that I was thrilled about being here myself. Given a choice between an unyielding wooden bench with just half an inch of well-worn cushion to protect my delicate posterior, or my nice comfy mattress with a continental quilt, I would probably opt for the bed and a Sunday lie-in. I shifted my knees to one side so Fergus could squeeze in, where he plonked himself down heavily, even going to the effort of folding his arms. That meant he was in a right strop.

I leaned down and whispered in his ear. 'How about we go for an ice cream after we're done here?'

His little face lit up. 'A Ninety-Nine?'

'Well, not sure where to get soft ice cream around here. Might have to be a Cornetto. Deal?'

He nodded, the scowl now banished and replaced with a huge cheesy grin. The way to a man's heart was through frozen confectionery.

Reverend Cackett appeared and stood before us, the hubbub from the congregation petering out until there was silence, save for the rustling of clothing, the odd self-conscious clearing of a throat, and the squeak of wooden benches. Most did not expect anything profound. His services were not known for their riveting content, and this lack of expectation was reflected in several of the faces around me. Most were clearly here as an obligation, or through habit, but a few stared at the vicar with rapt attention, awaiting the divine first words to pass his lips. He didn't cut an impressive figure. He had hair that had receded until it was well past his crown, a nose which was long and slightly crooked and eyes that I couldn't describe as anything but beady. If it weren't for the white alb and purple stole, he would look the most thoroughly unimpressive figure imaginable. I could easily conceive of him as a Whitehall civil servant, an anonymous and dreary man whom no one would ever think of looking at twice.

'We shall begin with hymn number 132: Thou Trespass Not unto the Lord,' he whined in a nasal tone.

The hum of whispers returned, tinged with an odd excitement. I glanced up at the small oak hymn board next to the pulpit. This was not Oh God Our Help in Ages Past, and from the confused looks and rustling of hymn books, it had taken everyone else by surprise as well. Everyone except the organist, it seemed, who struck the first notes of this ecclesiastical dirge. Wearily, the congregation dragged themselves to their feet and began to sing. The majority mumbled the words unenthusiastically, while the others made up for this by singing with gusto. I tried to straddle some middle ground. If I was on my own, I probably wouldn't have bothered, but for some unaccountable reason thought I should set an example for Fergus. Not that he needed any encouragement to perform. He sang merrily along, in a far more upbeat tone than was necessary or appropriate, but he was finally having fun.

As the hymn drew to a close, the vicar slowly, ploddingly ascended the steps to the pulpit and waited until there was silence and everyone had sat back down.

'There will now be a reading from Leviticus, Chapter Two.'

The passage was read by Jack Wimble, a solemn

and depressing section on the sins of stealing. Considering what I had recently learned about him, Jack Wimble was not someone I thought in a position to lecture on morality. Once he was finished and back in his seat, there was another hymn, this time the slightly more upbeat The Day Thou Gavest Lord is Ended. It still wasn't exactly All Things Bright and Beautiful, but was a moderate improvement nonetheless. After this, we finally got to the sermon. It wasn't likely to be riveting stuff, but would afford the congregation a few minutes to relax. Well, relax as well as we could on hard wooden pews.

'Welcome, everyone,' Reverend Cackett began. 'It is good to see so many familiar faces on this troubling day, as well as some not so familiar.'

I could've sworn he had looked in my direction as he said this.

'I have to begin with some sad news.'

It was hardly news, I thought. There couldn't be a soul in the village who hadn't heard about Veronica's death.

'Last night, a crime was committed against this very church. Some of you may have noticed the broken lock on the door. St Luke's was broken into last night and a sacred golden cross stolen from my desk in the vestry. Also, my desk drawer was forced open and the contents ransacked. It saddens my heart to think that such criminals are in our midst, that we know these people, that they are our brothers and children. It saddens me to think that we have opened our hearts to these people, and they have betrayed our trust. They will be judged, not on this Earth, but by the Lord our God when the day comes. Stealing is not just a crime of men, but a crime against God.'

I sat there open mouthed as he spoke, as he vented his furious venom at these individuals. He didn't hold back, either, and I was pretty sure he wouldn't be averse to a beheading or two, just to ensure the lesson was well learned. Or at the very least, a good old public flogging. He must have been very fond of that cross.

'These criminals – these utter villains – will be judged by God, oh yes, and they will be deemed unworthy to enter the Kingdom of Heaven. You mark my words, this is a crime for which they will pay with their souls!' He paused, his hands gripping the sides of the pulpit, and I could see his knuckles whitened, the sinews in his hands stretched taut. He took several deep breaths as he attempted to regain his composure, and then continued in a more even tone.

A final hymn ended the service and a quite stunned congregation ambled slowly out of the church, not daring to speak in anything but the quietest of whispers until they were outside. Fergus had thoroughly enjoyed himself, and if they were all like that, I'm sure he wouldn't be so averse to returning. He and I shuffled along with the rest, stopping to have a few words with Reverend Cackett. He had calmed down now, the release of emotion the safety valve he needed.

'Fergs, how do you fancy taking another look at those skulls at the back of the church?'

A Jubilee Murder

He looked up at me, half delighted and half looking for a trap. Deciding to throw caution to the wind, he raced back to the narthex and pressed his face up against a glass display cabinet. I needed to speak to the vicar, and Fergus delaying things should give me the opportunity.

As parishioners slowly filed out, a sombre vicar wished them well one by one, taking some of the women's hands in his and giving them a swift blessing. A few people wished to speak briefly about church matters, while others were keen to know what part St Luke's would be playing in the jubilee celebrations that were to engulf the village tomorrow. All offered their condolences over the break-in and theft.

'Mum,' Fergus shouted down the aisle to me, and I quickly shushed him. He continued in a stage whisper that did no less to draw attention to himself. 'These skulls are six thousand years old! And the stones could've been there for *ten* thousand years!'

'That's great,' I whispered back, trying to keep him quiet, and failing to disguise how funny his inopportune enthusiasm was.

The last of the parishioners said their goodbyes to the clergyman, and he turned and slowly strolled down the church to speak to Fergus and me, hands clasped behind his back.

'Good day, Mrs… Campbell?'

'Cameron, Reverend. Catriona Cameron. And this little horror is my son, Fergus. I'm sorry for the noise. He gets a bit excited sometimes, don't you, Fergs?'

He smiled down at the boy and ruffled his ginger hair, in a way that Fergus hated but dutifully endured. 'Children are often oblivious to social conventions. It's good to see the both of you. Especially you, young man. We don't have nearly enough young people supporting the church these days.'

Reverend Cackett had a peculiar smell to him, like he was coated in plain, unperfumed soap. I imagined him scrubbing the sin from his body every night while he sat curled up in his tin bath, probably using Brillo pads to scour the corruption away. Okay, I seriously doubted he had a tin bath, but this was my weird imagination we're talking about.

As soon as he could drag himself away, Fergus went back to studying the exhibits on display and reading through the accompanying leaflets. The fragments of pottery didn't really interest him, but the flint tools did.

'What brings you to church this day, Catriona?' he asked, still staring at the boy.

'Oh, no particular reason. I suppose the death of Veronica Castle was a shock. It makes one… re-examine one's faith, don't you think?'

'I'm not sure I would put it quite like that, my dear. I find that my faith in the Almighty never wavers. My faith in humanity, on the other hand, is constantly shaken.'

'You mean the break-in last night?'

'That, amongst other things. To rob the house of God. It is a crime against the Lord Himself. As was what happened to Veronica. I have grave fears for her eternal

120

soul. She was clearly a troubled woman, with a troubled past. She chose to end her life, to be spared more torment. But that does not change the fact that to take one's own life is a sin. We are not owners of these bodies, merely custodians.'

'Indeed. I take it you knew her from when she was a teenager here?'

He gave me an odd, quizzical look. 'No, I'm afraid not. I did not become vicar of this parish until some years after she left. If I had been here, perhaps I would have been able to steer her from the path of corruption, as I have others.'

'I must say, I was surprised that you allowed Mr Wimble to do the reading today, what with his history with Veronica.'

He seemed startled. 'We all have episodes in our past that we would choose to do differently, if we had the chance. I'm sure you yourself have events that happened in Aberdeen that you would rather forget, eh?'

It was my turn to be taken aback. 'I'm sure I do.' What did he know of my past? And how did he know I was from Aberdeen, specifically? It was fairly obvious that I was from Scotland, but I doubted he could pinpoint the specific accent that accurately. Then again, I didn't know how much of a topic of village gossip I was. Possibly, more than I would be comfortable with.

The reverend continued. 'I'm sure no good can come of raking up the past, my dear. It was all so long ago. So long ago.'

'You're absolutely right. Sometimes my curiosity gets the better of me.'

'And there's no crime in being curious, isn't that so, young man?' he said to Fergus, who merely shrugged, knowing that something weird was going on but not having the foggiest idea what.

'Well, thank you for indulging me, Reverend,' I said, gathering up Fergus and pointing him down the aisle, 'but I think it's time we were going. We've taken up far too much of your time already.'

'Not at all. It's been a pleasure to meet you both properly at last. I hope we will see you on a more regular basis?'

'I hope so too. Oh, just one more thing,' I enquired in true Columbo fashion. 'Do you know what happened to the child?'

'The child?'

'Yes, Veronica was pregnant when she left. I was wondering what happened to the baby.'

'I-I'm sorry, no. I don't know what happened to her. Now, if you'll excuse me, I really am frightfully busy today.'

He strode past me and down the aisle, to disappear into the vestry and close the door quite firmly. What an extraordinary performance, I thought. But it confirmed that he knew more about Veronica's past than he was letting on.

Until that moment, I had not known that the infant had survived, or that the child was a "her".

Twelve

I walked out of the church into the dazzling midday sunshine, scrabbling with one hand to get my sunglasses over my eyes before the inevitable happened, while simultaneously gripping Fergus's hand firmly. Too firmly, it turned out.

'Ow, Mum. You're hurting,' he whined, and I realised I was clutching him fiercely, not wanting him to stray more than a couple of feet away from me.

The church possessed a modest austerity inside. Simple and stark, but with an archaic beauty, the air itself infused with great age. I should have relished being inside such a building, but I was relieved beyond measure to escape its confines. The vicar gave me the creeps at the best of times, and today he was positively threatening. Or maybe I was just being overly sensitive.

The sun beat down with a fierce intensity, casting little flickering shapes through the yew trees' leaves. Most of the cars had disappeared while I remained inside, men heading off to The Old Badger and The Blue Bell, most of the women heading home to work on Sunday lunches. In a couple of hours, Downscliffe would be enveloped in the aromas of roast beef and chicken, sage & onion stuffing and thick gravy and roast potatoes. My little man would be wanting the same, but right now was torn.

Ahead, the village's cricket team was practising, bowlers running in and launching grenades at nervous batsmen. They were determined that this time they would beat Highview Village. Three losses in a row rankled.

Taking up the space of three cars, a minibus was parked below the trees, with the words "Highview Village Cricket Club" stencilled onto the side. How they had shoehorned eleven cricketers into the back of this converted transit van, I would never know. It was only a ten-minute drive from their ground, down the ear-poppingly steep Highview Hill and through Downscliffe to today's venue, but it was not my idea of a perfect Sunday.

The men milled about the minibus, some sitting on the rear bumper, others lounging on the grass and picking at exposed tree roots. They looked most impressive in cream trousers and open necked shirts. Most also wore cream coloured V-necked jumpers casually slung over their shoulders. Each seemed to be quite young, and fit, and intimidating. Despite Downscliffe's determination to reverse the trend, I did not rate their chances against this team from Highview Village.

One of the opposition players caught my eye, his bright ginger hair almost glowing when the sun caught it.

He was tall, his jaw unnaturally square. I told myself it had to be fake. Men's jaws didn't really come that square. Not in real life. He looked over to me and squinted, holding a hand over his eyes to shield them from the relentless sunshine. Once his vision had cleared and he'd blinked away some of the spots on his retinas, he smiled and trotted over to me. There were muted whoops from his teammates and he waved them away with a shake of his palm.

'No fraternising with the enemy, there,' came a shout from one of them.

'PC Cropper,' I said with hands on hips.

'Sorry about that,' he said when he got to me, grinning like a schoolboy. 'It's what you get…' He turned back to the others: '…when you work with a bunch of idiots!'

'I didn't know you played cricket,' I commented. 'I certainly didn't have you down as working for the opposition.'

'I try to play every other weekend during the summer, whenever I'm not on duty.' He looked down. And down. And down, until his eyes finally fell on the nervous little boy at my side. 'And I'm guessing this must be your little brother?'

'No, she's my mum,' Fergus corrected him.

'Oh, right. And what might your name be, young man?'

'Fergus.'

'Oh, what a cracking name. Wish I had a name like

that. Mine's really boring. I'm Colin.' He held out a massive, frying pan-sized hand for Fergus to shake.

'This is actually Constable Cropper, Fergs. He's a policeman.'

'Are you going to arrest me?' Fergus asked. His eyes darted left and right. He could not have looked more shifty. I hoped he grew out of that before anyone taught him poker.

'I don't know, Master Fergus. Have you done anything wrong?'

The boy now looked quite wretched, convinced that the game was up and he was about to be carted off to prison. 'Well… the label on the soldier said 13p, but the lady in the shop said it was 15p. My mum only had 13p so I said we would come back later with the other 2p, but we never did.'

'Oh deary me,' Colin said, tutting. 'I had no idea I was dealing with such a hardened criminal. Where was this?'

'Duncan's sweet shop on Scotstown Road.'

The ace detective glanced at me in confusion and I whispered: 'Aberdeen.'

'Ah, right,' he said. 'Out of our area so I don't think I'll arrest you today. As long as you behave yourself from now on.'

Fergus nodded so hard I thought he might give himself mild brain damage. Colin looked back to me. 'Are you going to stay and watch the match?'

'We'd love to,' I said, only lying a little bit, 'but

we've got to be getting home. This wee criminal genius will be wanting his Sunday dinner.'

'And get an ice cream. You did promise,' Fergus reminded me, making sure that he wasn't going to miss out on his Cornetto.

'And an ice cream,' I reassured him.

'Oh, that's too bad. Thought you might like to see us demolish Downscliffe.'

'Well jings crivvens and help ma boab,' I grinned, but had no doubt he was probably right.

Colin pulled a pained expression. 'And there I was, thinking we spoke the same language.'

'Hey, CCC, skip's off for the toss,' shouted one of the others. Another member of the Highview Village team was striding out into the middle of the pitch, where the Downscliffe captain and two umpires were waiting.

'CCC?' I asked.

He groaned. 'Yeah, it's… Cropper, the Copper-top Copper. Bit of a tongue-twister. Wouldn't recommend it when you're drunk.'

'Hence the abbreviation,' I nodded.

'Mum, isn't that what Auntie Debbie called him?' a little voice queried.

'Haud yer weesht, Fergus!' I hissed, but Colin just laughed.

'Clearly, there are never any secrets with a kid around. I'll ask "Auntie Debbie" about that next time I see her.'

'Please do,' I said with a hint of malice. 'She'd be

mortified.' I leaned a little closer to him and lowered my voice, not that there was anyone but Fergus anywhere close to being in earshot. 'Did you manage to speak to your CID friends about you know what?'

The smile wavered for a moment. 'Yeah, not good news, I'm afraid. They're not going to go for it. Not enough evidence to investigate further.'

'And they're not going to get any more evidence if they don't investigate,' I complained, having expected nothing more but still feeling a twinge of disappointment.

'How about you? Uncovered anything else that might be of use?'

I shrugged. 'Quite a bit of background stuff, but nothing incriminating against anyone. It seems that our late friend Veronica had quite the history in this village. I mean, we're talking an affair way back, a pregnancy, secrets—'

'Blackmail, deceit and dastardly skulduggery, that sort of thing?'

'Highly likely. There are a handful of people who were around in 1948 when it all happened, and I'm just starting to uncover some facts.'

'Well you be careful. Stories that get buried are buried for a reason. People have secrets and if you go digging up the past, certain individuals may not like it. I don't want you putting yourself in any danger.'

'Aw, are you getting all protective of me?' I teased.

'No, but if you get yourself murdered, I'm the one that's going to be left with the paperwork.'

'You're all heart, PC Cropper. About Veronica,' I said, hesitating a moment. 'Was there anything in her hoose that looked suspicious to you? Anything on her body?'

He shook his head, clearly wishing there was. 'No, absolutely nothing. No signs of a struggle, no ornaments knocked over. As for the body...' He glanced down at Fergus, who had lost interest in him and was watching proceedings play out in the centre of the pitch, and whispered to me. 'As for the body, CID conducted a rudimentary exam, as did the Home Office pathologist, but there was nothing obvious that made it look suspicious. There was no damage to her clothing and no sign of defensive marks to her person. No scratches or bruises to indicate she had gone unwillingly, and the wound to her neck was consistent with a death by short drop hanging.'

I nodded. I didn't know how it had happened; how an assailant had killed her without leaving any physical traces, but I was convinced that it was a murder. 'Thanks. I haven't a clue who it was, or how they did it, but I know she didn't kill herself.'

'I believe you. Just be careful, you hear? And remember, stay away from Miss Castle's house. No getting caught sneaking around in there.'

'Oh don't worry, I'll make sure we're not caught.'

Colin rolled his eyes heavenward and shook his head. 'I don't want to know.'

'Heads!' came a shout from the centre of the pitch,

and I saw a shiny coin flicked into the air, to come rapidly spinning back to Earth and land in the grass. The two team captains and umpires peered in to look at it, and there were nods all round. The captains shook hands and exchanged a few words. With a languid point of the Highview captain's finger, the rest of the team roused themselves.

'Looks like we're fielding,' Colin said, and I got the feeling he was just a tiny bit disappointed.

'Okay, good luck. Are you a bowler?'

'Wicketkeeper,' he said as he turned to dash back to the minibus. 'With hands like these, I couldn't be anything else.' He waved them in the air like Al Jolson, and I half expected him to launch into a rendition of My Mammy.

'Can we stay and watch, Mum?' Fergus asked, getting fidgety.

'No sweetheart, we've got to get home and cook you some dinner. And maybe we could do some more work on your costume. Besides, you and me need to go and get some ice creams, don't we?' In the space of a few seconds, I saw his face go from crushing disappointment to grudging acceptance to excited delight.

We did stay for a couple of minutes, just to watch the Highview Village team stroll out onto the pitch to take up their positions.

As I turned away, I caught a glimpse of the church doorway, and of the shadowy figure lurking there. The alb was gone now, and he was left in full black cassock. He stared at me for a few more seconds, before retreating inside again.

I glanced back at the field as the two Downscliffe batsmen walked nervously out to take up their positions. It did give me cause for a small chuckle. They were going to get slaughtered.

Thirteen

Steam filled the kitchen, the windows running with condensation despite the back door being open. Coming from the wireless was the distorted jangle of Steely Dan's East St Louis Toodle-Oo as Annie Nightingale's Request Show started. This Radio One programme had not quite reached the dizzying levels of popularity of Ceilidh Hour on Northeast Scotland Community Radio, but it was certainly good enough for me as I slaved over the Sunday dinner.

I took a peek inside the oven, opening the door just a crack and blinking away the hot steam that erupted from within. The joint of beef was sizzling away nicely, its surface a rich brown and the aroma pervading the whole house like a warm, comforting blanket. The meat was as done as it was going to be, so it was time to take it out to rest until carving time. My oven gloves were a garish orange and yellow flowery pattern on the outside, all daisies and buttercups and dandelions, but the insides were charred black from a thousand burnt offerings. I plonked the roasting dish on the counter top with a crash. As much as I loved my happily mad oven gloves, they had worn to the point that every time I used them, I risked serious injury. If I were arrested, the police would think that I was trying to burn off my own fingerprints. Maybe I could re-line them to stave off the inevitable? Or just cremate them completely and be done with it.

The roast potatoes were still sizzling away, the fat bubbling in the dish as they slowly browned. Yorkshire puddings were on the top shelf of the oven and resolutely refusing to show any signs of life, languidly lying there like Liz Taylor after a heavy night on the town. Runner beans and carrots were prepared and the water heating. The skirlie was mixed and ready to heat in the pan. Everything was ready and, with the exception of the recalcitrant Yorkshire puddings, it all seemed to be coming along nicely.

I took a sip of my tattie wine. This was my second glass, and I could already feel it was having an effect. Cooking is always so much more enjoyable with a little alcohol to lubricate proceedings.

A roast dinner always seemed to consist of two hours of relaxed preparation, culminating in ten minutes of blind panic. This would be the worst possible time for an interruption, so naturally that was the moment the doorbell rang. I very quickly checked that nothing was about to boil over, burn or actually catch fire, and shouted down the hall towards Fergus's room. 'Fergs, get your bahookie out here; I need you to stir the gravy.'

A Three Villages Mystery

There was a crash of something going over, and I guessed it was the tower of cassette tapes that had been precariously piled on his chest of drawers. He came racing from the room and skidded to a halt some way into the kitchen, his socks a little more slippery than he had expected. He held a small cardboard pyramid in one hand, from which he slurped a defrosting Jubbly orange.

I pointed to the smallest saucepan on the hob. 'Get stirring, loon. I'll see who that is.'

I strode down the hall and recognised the silhouette through the frosted glass in the front door. Turquoise trousers and a baggy cheesecloth top meant there was only one person it could be.

'Wotcha,' Debbie said, a big cheesy grin on her face but her eyes looking weary.

'Hi trouble,' I welcomed her. 'You coming in, quine?'

'Bad time?'

'Terrible.'

'Then I don't mind if I do.'

I hustled through to the kitchen, where Fergus was concentrating on stirring the gravy in the pan. The lids of the other pans were rattling away, bubbles spilling from the rims and dribbling down the sides to sizzle extravagantly in the flames. I adjusted the heat on the gas burners and set the lids at a more jaunty angle. The radio was still playing, the song having moved on to Tie a Yellow Ribbon Round the Old Oak Tree.

'Smells great, Caty. Your cooking always does,'

Debbie said with a fake note of jealousy.

'Aye, right up until I burn the lot. You want to take over gravy duty from Fergs?'

'Sure. Leave it to your top two staff to handle the most important job.'

Fergus handed her the wooden spoon. 'You have to do it in a figure of eight to stop the middle bit sticking,' he advised her earnestly, and even waited for a few moments to make sure she was doing it properly, before scurrying off to his room at the far end of the hall.

'Are you staying for some?' I asked as I gently fried the onions for the skirlie.

'No, flying visit, really. Just needed five minutes away from Satan's unholy anti-cherubs and Captain Useless.'

'Oh no, don't tell me they played up?'

'You know my plan to take them to the park, get them to spend the afternoon running around to wear them out? Well, the first part of that worked out fine. They must've done a dozen circuits of the park, and it's a big park. Plus they were up and down trees like a pair of demented squirrels. Did it wear them out?'

'I'm guessing not.'

'Did it heck as like. All it did was get them more worked up. And then, to make the evening just that little bit more special, Tony gets an emergency call out. Can you believe it? Eleven o' clock on a Saturday night, and he's off fixing some dozy bint's leccy supply. By the time he got home, the moment was kind of gone.' She stared disconsolately into the swirling gravy as she stirred, absently following Fergus's instructions and following a figure eight pattern.

'You know what you need? I asked.

'A psychiatrist?'

'Almost. A good old-fashioned girls' night in. Fergs can be in bed by nine-ish. We can have a bit of telly. A bit of wine.'

'A bit?'

'A *lot* of wine. I think you need it. And a bit of adult conversation, without kids or electricians. Fancy that, quine?'

'Oh, hell yes! If I don't get out of that house for a few hours soon, the rozzers will find three more dead bodies down this road.'

I gave her an affirmative nod and took a sip of my tattie wine. 'Did you want a glass of this now?'

'No, I'll just take a swig of yours.' She held out her hand and took the glass. Well, it was more like snatched, but we won't quibble. Suffice it to say, this was a woman in dire need of some winding down.

The music changed again to a bit of Suzi Quatro and Devil Gate Drive.

'Oh, we've *got* to play this tonight,' Debbie almost shouted, passing the almost empty glass back to me. She stood there for a few seconds, eyes closed and mouthing the words to the song with a sneer twisting her face. Miming with serious attitude. I chuckled at this. My friend, the would-be rock chick. In turquoise trousers.

'Or…' she said, the wooden spoon slowing almost to a standstill. I cleared my throat and looked pointedly down at the gravy pan, and she resumed. 'Instead of going up to Veronica's house tomorrow, we could go tonight. You know, under cover of darkness.'

I was in the process of draining the carrots when she dropped this little bombshell. To sneak in there at night might be a better plan. There was less likelihood of running into any reporters and the like if we went late, and it was obviously much less likely that we would be seen by nosy neighbours. It would mean leaving Fergus on his own for half an hour or so, but he was a sensible boy and could usually be trusted not to get into any trouble.

'What about it?' Debbie pressed. 'You think it's a good idea?'

'Aye, I do,' I said slowly. 'In fact, I think it's an excellent idea. Right, let's do it.'

She looked shocked. 'I had a good idea? Groovy. Perhaps I should make a note in my diary.'

'You'll have to learn how to write first.'

'Oh yeah, there's always some little fly in the ointment, isn't there?'

'The best laid plans of Debs and men,' I agreed, giving the skirlie a stir.

'I'll wear some dark threads. You do the same.'

'This is rapidly turning into a Pink Panther movie,' I quipped as I swung open the door to the oven, steam and the heady scent of well-roasted tatties spilling out. Debbie stared at the tray with covetous envy. 'Oh, they look slammin'. I'm divorcing Tony and marrying you.'

'I'm not sure that would work out,' I laughed. 'Now, if you're staying, get an extra set of knives and forks. If you're going, later days, sister.'

'Okay, okay, I know when I've outstayed my welcome. Check ya later, buttercup.'

She gave an extravagant wave as she disappeared down the hallway and shouted a goodbye to Fergus. A few seconds later, after some furious cursing as she battled with the front door, the whirlwind known as Debbie Dugdale was gone.

Fourteen

nce Debbie and dinner were out of the way, I had that most peculiar experience of something called free time. It was becoming a rarer and rarer occurrence, and left me in a bit of a quandary as to how to fill this void – for about five seconds. For me nowadays, there really was no such thing as free time, just moments of transition between bouts of blind panic. I still had Fergus's Doctor Who costume to finish, although I had to admit, when he tried it on the night before, he had looked pretty darned good, almost as if Tom Baker had been washed on too high a temperature and had shrunk. All I had to do was dye the hat and it was ready. Okay, the wig smelled like his Great Aunt Moira, but that was a necessary evil.

Half an hour later, a now burgundy hat was drying in the linen cupboard. Next on the never-ending to-do list was Her Majesty's chocolate biscuit cake. Strictly speaking, as I was no longer participating in the baking competition as a contestant, I didn't actually *need* to make a cake. However, I thought it would add to my meagre credibility if I did. Some of the entrants might have read one or two of my cookbooks, but none of them had firsthand experience of my practical baking efforts, except perhaps a slice of "stodgy mess of confectionery excess" bread pudding in The Old Badger. I was just this weird Scottish woman who'd come in and been made a judge by default, unlike the previous holder of the position who had her very own show on the telly. Okay, it was only lowly old Southern Television, but better than a couple of books from a niche publisher.

As much as I would have loved to settle down in front of the telly and happily doze off while Norman Wisdom and Margaret Rutherford engaged in all manner of "hilarious" antics in BBC 1's Sunday afternoon movie, I knew I had to make this cake.

I settled down at the kitchen table, stifling yawn after yawn as I carefully broke up rich tea biscuits into small pieces. The recipe was simple enough, but was one of those where the trick was in the care with which it is put together. It wouldn't require much skill, just time and patience.

An hour later, the mixture had been pressed into a pair of cake rings and they were now chilling in the fridge. A feeling of unease had descended upon me as I worked, a nagging little sensation of butterflies that fluttered away inside. Poking around in Veronica's car had been one thing. Its top was open so filching about under the seat wasn't exactly unlawful entry. Okay, it might have been unlawful entry in the eyes of the law, but there was no harm done. Not really. Now we were planning on breaking into her house and ransacking the place. Well, maybe not ransacking it. More like letting ourselves in with a key and having a quiet snoop about. Putting it like that, it didn't sound so bad, but if Debbie's rozzers turned up and caught us in the act, we would be, as the saying goes, well and truly banged to rights. I kept telling myself that it was for a good cause, that it was to give Veronica a little justice, so the world would know that she had not killed herself, but died by another's hand.

Why did I care? It wasn't as if we were close. I couldn't stand the woman, and I'm sure she must have felt the same way about me. I just didn't like the idea of someone literally getting away with murder. I was also not thrilled with the idea of a killer walking around and potentially being a danger to Fergus. And to me, for that matter, but he always came first.

When Fergus appeared in the early evening, hungry and rubbing his tummy for extra effect, I knocked him up a corned beef and mustard sandwich, with a couple of Penguin biscuits for afters. By nine o' clock he had taken himself off to bed to read. "Android Planet" may not exactly have been Tolstoy, but I was happy that he was reading something. Anything is better than nothing, and fortunately he loved books.

Half an hour later, the doorbell rang and I could see a shadowy figure beyond the frosted glass. The door opened on the third try, the catch not drawing back quite far enough to allow it to unlatch, so it required a fair bit of rattling, coaxing and not a few choice expletives before it opened.

'Wotcha,' Debbie whispered, surreptitiously looking right and left like a big, black-clad Secret Squirrel. 'Are we still on for tonight?'

'Aye, I think we are. Are you sober?'

'Of course I am. The very idea. Are you going to let me in, then? I think I could do with a little potato wine bravery shot.'

I moved out of the way and ushered her in. I wasn't sure whether I was happy that Debbie was as nervous as I was, or whether it just reinforced my own anxiety.

In the kitchen, she plonked herself down onto one of the stiff-backed chairs, while I retrieved a new bottle of tattie wine from the squeaky cupboard. She hadn't been kidding, and was clad head to toe in black and looked like a groupie for The Stranglers. Black slacks, thin black sweater. Even black boots. Me, I had opted for dark blue jeans and a loose, chunky knit jumper. The chocolate brown one with the ridiculously baggy sleeves and which practically came down to my knees. At a push, I dare say I could've worn it as a dress.

I filled Debbie in on all that I had learned about Veronica and her past over the previous twenty-four hours. She listened with eyes going wide, eyebrows going up and, on occasion, a hand coming up to her chest. Debbie had a flair for the dramatic.

'It smells of chocolate in here,' she said, her nose

twitching. 'What have you been up to?'

'A cake for the contest tomorrow.'

'Ooh, can I try some?'

'It's for the contest *tomorrow*,' I repeated, enunciating the last word with theatrical clarity for effect. 'Besides, it's not finished yet. I've gotten a bit behind, so I'll have to finish it tonight.'

Debbie pulled a face. In her eyes, there were few crimes more heinous than denying her chocolate. 'You realise I'm going to be up here first thing tomorrow morning to get some, don't you?'

'I said it's for *tomorrow*!'

'And I'll have some *tomorrow*. I also happen to know that you would have made a spare for testing. So don't give me any of that "not to be eaten until the contest" malarkey, Catriona Cameron.'

I had to break into a chuckle at this point. Debbie was far smarter than she often made out, and predictably my subterfuge was revealed. 'Okay, okay, I give up. There's no chocolate coating yet, but we can try some when we get back. That good enough, Inspector Dugdale?'

'It'll have to be. Now, are we driving up to Veronica's house?'

'No, I figured it would look suspicious if Ernie was seen in her driveway late at night. We can walk up there.'

'And what if someone sees us?'

'We've had a drink and we're out for a late evening stroll to clear our nappers.'

A Three Villages Mystery

Debbie nodded. 'Sounds plausible enough. You do have quite a reputation for… you know…' She put thumb and forefinger together and raised them to her lips in the internationally recognised gesture for "drinkie-drinkie".

'Me? You could practically float the QE2 in what you drink on the average Saturday night, and you have the nerve to accuse me!'

She laughed. I laughed. In fact, we both laughed far more than was strictly warranted, and I'm sure nervousness played a role in this.

I stood, feeling a weariness in my legs. It had been a long day of walking, standing, kneeling etc. But this tired achiness was down to tension, plain and simple.

Debbie quaffed the last of her wine, gazing longingly at the rest of the bottle, and I could almost see the internal monologue going on inside her head. Another glass would be a mistake, she was thinking. Afterwards, we could polish off the bottle. But for now we needed to remain mostly clear-headed.

She pushed the glass away and stood. 'Right, are we doing this thing?' she demanded, and I knew there was no more putting it off.

'We certainly are. Time to go. Hopefully they'll let us be cellmates in Holloway after we're convicted.'

Fifteen

arkness was now absolute, save for the sparkling starlight that shone down on the village like a thousand little torch beams. Some light spilled from living rooms as we crept uneasily along the lane.

In the distance I could hear the never-ending rumble of traffic on the M20. The motorway was just a mile from where we were as the crow flies, but always seemed much further off. At night, it felt like an artery, the constant stream of lights scurrying along the road its blood. To some, the motorway was an ugly scar across the ancient landscape, the noise an unwelcome reminder of the modern world encroaching, but to me it had been a comfort. I loved it here, in this most quaint and picturesque of English villages, but after dark, when the inhabitants were tucked away safely in their homes, the shadows could become unnerving. If it weren't for the companionship of the motorway, the silence would be absolute, the isolation all but intolerable.

A handful of birds still chirped in the trees,

punctuated by the squeaks of bats darting about overhead, and every now and then we would catch the sound of a television in a living room. It was hard to imagine that in another twelve hours or so, the village would be a bustling, cheering, laughing arena of life and happiness as the jubilee celebrations got under way. There was no bunting on Ashfield Lane; the Jubilee Committee had not budgeted for decorations to extend this far from the village centre, but several of the houses had hung their own decorations. Bunting, flags, pictures of the Queen and balloons in red, white and blue covered some houses, while others had ignored the festival completely.

Tonight, we were in luck; we didn't encounter a single car on our walk to Veronica's house. This wasn't unusual. Ashfield Lane was not a cut-through to anywhere else, the only people using it being the residents themselves. This late in the evening, it was common for half an hour or more to elapse without any sign of a car or person on the lane.

Veronica Castle's house was, as I'd expected, in complete darkness. The curtains were drawn and every window appeared closed.

'Do you think there's an alarm?' Debbie whispered.

'I don't know. I hadn't thought of that. It's possible, though. She was away a lot to Southampton for filming her programme, so she may have had an alarm put in.'

'Great, something else to worry about.'

'What should we do?' I asked uncertainly.

In the dim light of the stars I saw her shrug. 'We go

in anyway. Your mate, PC Gingernut practically told us to, and I think he would've mentioned if there was an alarm, wouldn't he?'

That was a good point. As always, my rapier-like intellect hadn't let me down. 'You're right.'

'And if an alarm does go off, we scarper. Leg it back to your place and stay there until we're too drunk to care.'

This was a plan I could enthusiastically endorse.

The driveway was noisy, crunchy gravel, so we kept to the grass, sneakily tiptoeing along in a fashion that would've looked hilarious to anyone who might be watching. The house with its bizarre trio of slanted roofs was set well back from the lane. A double garage was off to one side, joined to the main part of the house. There was no sign of the Spitfire, which Constable Cropper had informed me had been returned to the house, so I imagined it was tucked away inside the garage now.

For the first time, I wondered who the recipient of all this would be. There may or may not have been a daughter, but I knew of no other family other than poor old Wally Moore, and I doubted he would have a claim to the estate. If there was no will, the house and everything in it would probably go to the state.

'We should look for a will while we're in there,' I whispered as we stood in front of the house. 'If there is one—'

'It could finger exactly who murdered Her Ladyship,' Debbie interrupted. 'I know, I thought of that earlier today. And then promptly forgot about it. Thanks for reminding me.'

At first glance, it looked like there was no way through to the back garden except through the house, which, of course, was locked. That was why we needed to get around the back. However, there was a very narrow alleyway to the right of the garage, with a rusted wrought iron gate blocking the way. Fortunately, there was no padlock on it, or that would have ended our illicit adventure then and there. I slid back the catch, which screeched like an owl caught in a mincer. The noise made me wince, and I expected half the lane to have heard it. We held our breath for several seconds, waiting to hear if dogs started barking nearby, or if one of the neighbours would come out to investigate. We heard nothing, save for the constant rumble of motorway traffic that echoed across the valley and the trickle of water from an overflow pipe nearby.

'Think you could do that a bit louder next time?' Debbie whispered.

'Sorry, I forgot my cat burglar kit with the 3-in-1 oil,' I snapped back, and pulled a face that made zero impact in the darkness. I pushed at the gate and heard it begin to squeak.

'Shush,' hissed Debbie.

'It's not like I'm doing it on purpose!' I wrapped my fingers around the wrought ironwork and lifted as I pushed, and this seemed to lessen the noise until the gate was open wide enough for us to get through.

We crept along the narrow space, the garage on one

side, a high brick wall on the other. Cobwebs brushed my cheeks and lips and eyelids, and I frantically wiped them away. I wasn't keen on spiders at the best of times, and this was just an added torture. I should have let Debbie go first. She was weird, one of those peculiar people who didn't mind beasties. More than once, I had phoned her in the evening to get her to come up to my place and get rid of a particularly large specimen. It made me shudder just to think about it, and I furiously ruffled my hair to dislodge any would-be hitchhikers.

We emerged into the back garden, which looked a creepy dull grey in the starlight. There was nothing in the least bit remarkable about it. The grass had been trimmed a week or two earlier and a quite dilapidated greenhouse was on one side, its panes opaque with grime, lichens and cobwebs. There were bushes further down, but beyond that, I could see nothing. Fortunately, our eyes were becoming quite adjusted to the low-light conditions, and I could make out a few details in the immediate area. There was a flagstone patio just outside the back door, and a garden table with two chairs.

'The key must be under one of those,' I muttered, pointing to a pair of garden urns by the back door, and gave the nearest one a push. 'They're not light. If I rock it to one side, you get your torch and look underneath. Okay?'

'Right on, sister.'

I used both hands to put pressure on the urn until I felt it begin to shift. There was a grinding crunch as I levered it over, tiny shards of gravel protesting, but soon it was at a thirty-degree angle and Debbie could get down on her haunches and shine a torch under there. As I watched, a handful of creepy crawlies came scurrying from underneath having been rudely disturbed. They were mostly earwigs and slaters. At least, slaters are what I called them. In this specific area of Kent they were known as cheesy bugs. Just about everyone else in the world called them woodlice.

'Bingo,' Debbie whispered, and emerged with a shiny mortice lock key which glinted in the light from her torch.

As carefully as I could, I returned the urn to its upright position, there being a dull thud as it touched the ground. Debbie looked most pleased with herself, and bustled over to the back door and tried the key in the lock. I was mildly jealous when I saw that it slid in and turned easily, and the door catch was released. Why couldn't my door open as easily?

We waited a few seconds for a burglar alarm to pierce the night, but mercifully there was nothing, just the sound of a tap dripping in the kitchen.

'Let's get in there,' I mumbled, more nervous than ever out in the open.

I fumbled in my pocket for my own little Ever Ready torch, fingers wrapping around the smooth plastic. The beam was pitifully weak, but that was fine by me. Less chance of us being seen from the road. It was unlikely that a passing car would notice torch lights inside the darkened property, but there were a lot of dog walkers around, and some would go out at the most peculiar times.

We edged cautiously inside, weak beams from the torches dancing over walls and kitchen cabinets. It was immaculately kept, every device in pristine condition, every surface cleaned to within an inch of its life. I knew this wasn't Veronica's studious hard work, but that of her cleaner.

'I never thought it would be so creepy in here,' Debbie whispered. 'If we see the ghost of Veronica, I am outta here.'

'You and me both, quine.'

'Do you think there's anyone else here?' she breathed, shining her torch over work surfaces, kettle and toaster reflecting the light back.

'The house is pitch dark; why would there be anyone else here?'

'Well in that case, why are we whispering?' she whispered.

This was one of those moments where you realise how ridiculous you're behaving. 'It's a fair point. I'm not great when it comes to all this cloak and dagger stuff, okay?'

I shone my torch through the kitchen doorway and into the living room. The floor was uncarpeted, the walls clad in pine panels stretching right up to the angled ceiling. The house had clearly been designed in the sixties, with bold angled roofs and asymmetric rooms. The lounge was large, but sparsely furnished. The centre of the space was taken up by three large sofas arranged into a square horseshoe. As I shone the light around, the beam picked out details: a large television on a nondescript cabinet against one wall, a hi-fi system against another, a shelf with various awards, a handful of abstract paintings. There was nothing cosy about it, nothing that made it feel like a home. There were no photographs of family or loved ones, no sentimental keepsakes. Being here now, late at night and in the dark, with the threat of discovery hanging over us, it did not lend itself to promoting a feeling of relaxed contentment, but I was sure that this room would feel unwelcoming in any circumstance.

'This must be where it happened,' Debbie muttered. She wasn't whispering now, but also there was no longer any hint of levity in her voice.

I followed where she was looking, her torch shining into the hallway. The ceiling here was vertiginously high, stretching at least fifteen feet into the air. The torch beam carved a path upwards until we caught sight of the overhead light fitting. Whatever shade there once was had disappeared, just six inches of cable ending in a bare lightbulb. From this hung another cable, tied into a loop which had been cut. We stared at it dumbly for several seconds, imagining what the scene must have looked like when poor old Wally Moore had wandered in and discovered his niece. To one side was a small table with a telephone, and next to this was a stiff-backed chair.

'That must be where the police cut her down,' I said,

waving my torch beam at where the noose had been severed.

'And she must have climbed up onto that chair,' Debbie said. 'Head in the noose, then kicked the chair away. Classic.'

I looked across at the chair, which had been put back in place by the police, and then up at the broken loop. I frowned. 'There's something not quite right here.'

'There's something *seriously* not right here,' Debbie blurted. 'We're looking at the noose where a woman killed herself. Or someone else killed her. One or the other, but nothing about this is right.'

'How tall was Veronica?' I asked.

'I don't know. Five-five, five-six?'

'That's what I thought.' I pulled the chair away from the wall and placed it under the light fitting. 'Debs, how tall are you?'

'Five foot seven.'

'Okay, stand on the chair.'

'You've got to be kidding. That's just—'

'I know, it's sick and creepy. But just do it, would you?'

She sighed, pausing for a moment before shaking her head and climbing onto the chair. It wobbled a little as it took her full weight, its joints creaking.

'Veronica was wearing heels, so stand on tiptoes,' I instructed.

Debbie did as I asked and I stepped back, shining my torch at her neck, and then up at the noose.

'Well?' she demanded, dropping so that her heels touched the chair again, before raising up once more, eliciting a fresh series of squeaks from the chair. 'Are you satisfied now?'

'Can you reach up and put that noose around your neck?'

'What? Are you—'

'Just do it. Please.'

She harrumphed theatrically, but felt for the cable nonetheless, her torch beam dancing wildly on the walls as she fumbled with the two ends of the cut cord. Debbie tugged at them, pulled them tight, but did not get them to go around her neck.

'Wow, that's totally freaky.' Debbie looked down at me and winced as I shone the torch in her face. 'She couldn't have hanged herself. The wire wouldn't reach her neck.'

I took her hand and helped her awkwardly down off the chair. 'I'd say that cord is at least four inches too short,' I said. Oddly, I didn't feel triumphant or elated in any way, just sad. A wave of melancholy washed over me. I somehow wished she *had* committed suicide. If her life had been that awful, then death would have given her some release and ended her suffering. But she hadn't wanted to die. Someone had taken her life from her. Regardless of my personal animosity toward Veronica, she had deserved to live, and this right had been taken away from her.

'We need to tell your boyfriend about this,' Debbie

said, looking up at the cable again.

'He's not my boyfriend.'

'Of course not, but we need to tell him.'

'I will. Hopefully I'll see him tomorrow at the jubilee. This establishes she didn't kill herself, but gets us no closer to finding out who *did* kill her.'

'Something to do with her past,' Debbie mused. 'It has to be that. Jack Wimble, do you think? She was an embarrassment and a reminder of past indiscretions. Could he have killed her over that?'

'But why now? If that were the case, why not do it two years ago when she first came back to the village?'

'Okay, so who else do we have? The vicar? Frankly, I think he's guilty simply because he gives me the creeps.'

'And me. It could be him. I can't think of a motive off the top of my head, but that doesn't mean there isn't one. Just that we haven't found it yet. Same goes for Barry Huckstep, the tractor driver. He creeped me right out, but I can't think of what his motive might be. I mean it's not as if he and Veronica moved in the same social circles.'

'Jack Wimble could have put him up to it.'

'But then we come back again to why did Jack want her dead now?'

I froze. A noise came from the living room. It was only quiet, barely audible, but I definitely heard a bump. So did Debbie, who stared at me with her eyes practically out on stalks, mouth wide open as if she'd just sat on a drawing pin.

'Torch,' I mouthed, and she fumbled with the switch

on the little gadget. I switched mine off as well. Neither of us moved, immobilised by blind terror.

There was another sound, a kind of scratching noise, like an animal clawing at something. A cat? No, I was sure Veronica hadn't owned any pets.

A louder thump was accompanied by a grunt. That wasn't the grunt of an animal. That came from a human being.

It was a man's grunt.

I placed a hand on Debbie's shoulder and felt her jump. I think it was only because she was so paralysed with terror that she didn't scream. As gently as I could, I moved her aside so I could peek around the corner and into the living room.

That was when I saw the shadowy figure.

Sixteen

s I peered around the doorway, I saw him there, crouching on the floor like a predator preparing to pounce on its victim. The only light in the room was what came in from the wide patio doors, but on this moonless night it was feeble. All I could see was the figure's silhouette, a phantom that only became visible when he moved.

I felt Debbie's hand on my arm, and her body just behind me as she poked her head out gingerly to see him for herself. 'Is it the police?' she whispered almost inaudibly in my ear.

'I don't think the police would come in through the window,' I murmured back.

The figure straightened up and tossed something onto the nearest sofa. I realised it was a duffel bag, its contents clearly quite weighty. They made a jangling noise of metal clanging together.

I ran my fingers along the wall, feeling for a light switch. From the silhouette of his legs, the man looked slim and rangy, and I thought – hoped – that if it came to a physical confrontation, Debbie and I together might be able to overpower him. Might. Why was he here? Was he the murderer, come to retrieve some incriminating piece of evidence? An opportunistic burglar, perhaps? I wanted to see who we were dealing with. I *needed* to see him, this darkness making me far more nervous than the intruder himself. The *other* intruder, I corrected myself. We were hardly here by invitation, were we? My fingers stopped at a raised panel, and I felt the cool plastic of two rocker switches. I flicked them both on with an audible double click.

The living room was suddenly bathed in dazzling, blinding light which, somewhat predictably, tickled the back of my nose and I instantly erupted in a fit of completely uncontrolled sneezes.

'Achoo!'

'Don't move, sucker,' I heard Debbie shout.

'Achoo!'

'Just stay…'

'Achoo!'

'…where you are.'

'Achoo!'

'Oh, close the shades, Caty!'

'Who are you two?' the man demanded.

Through watery eyes I tried to make out the intruder. He was tall and almost painfully thin, dressed in wide bottomed blue jeans, a sailor style stripey t-shirt and black leather bikers' jacket. His hair was long and dark brown in a shag "style". He could, for all the world, have been a reject from Led Zeppelin. He was also very young. I'd put him at no older than sixteen or maybe seventeen at a push.

'You the police?' he asked, his eyes dancing from the dark-haired woman giving the orders, to the ginger snot factory holding her sleeve against her nose.

'Do we look like the police?' Debbie asked, but continued without waiting for an answer. 'What are you doing breaking in here?'

'I wasn't breaking in.'

'You came in through the window.'

'Yeah, but I didn't break it.'

I scrabbled in my pocket for a handkerchief. It had the same little flowery patterns at the corners as the one from the other day, but I swear it was clean. In a less than ladylike fashion, I blew my nose loudly, sounding like the QE2 coming into port.

'Normal people come in through the door, buster,' Debbie continued.

'Never mind that,' I said, dabbing the hankie at my watery eyes, 'just tell us what you're doing here. And what's in the duffel bag.'

He looked down at the bag, suddenly looking decidedly shifty. 'Nothing.'

'It looks very heavy for a lot of nothing,' I pressed. The boy looked ready to be sick, but I didn't sense any threat from him. He seemed more like an errant schoolboy dragged before the headmaster.

A Three Villages Mystery

Debbie didn't wait for him to answer, and went over to look in the bag. It jangled as it was turned upright and she peered inside. When she looked up at me, she was grinning. 'I think we've found our prime suspect.'

I was too perplexed to respond, and just looked at her with head cocked to one side. 'You mean he killed—'

'No, not *that* crime.' She pulled out a tin of Fresh Fayre baked beans and held it up for me to see clearly. 'There's another half a dozen cans of these in here, and a tin opener. Got a fondness for beans, have we?'

He stumbled backwards until he hit the wall, and slid down it like a balloon being deflated. Now he looked like a dead spider, his limbs folded up. 'I'm sorry,' he muttered, and I could hear his voice breaking. 'It was supposed to be a joke. You know, I was just trying to fake people out.'

The young man was desperately trying to be cool, I realised, but was just a goofball.

'What's your name, Che Guevara?' I asked, wiping my recalcitrant nose one more time and stuffing the soaking handkerchief back in my pocket.

'Sean,' he muttered, and looked up at us sheepishly. 'Sean Pemble.'

'Pemble?' I repeated. 'But that's… You attacked your own house with baked beans?'

He nodded.

'Are you a complete idiot?' Debbie asked incredulously.

'I must be. I can't stand my parents. They're so

stupid.'

'Whereas you're clearly the brainy one in the family,' Debbie persisted. She wasn't going to give him a moment's respite.

'It started as a joke, you dig? Then I saw something. Something real bad.'

I strolled over to him and crouched down on my haunches, attempting to peer into his eyes, but he couldn't meet my gaze for more than an instant. 'What did you see, Sean?'

His eyes flicked up at me, just for a moment, before looking down again at the hard wooden floor. 'I was down at the church. I was gonna bean it. Thought that would be cool, you dig? Thought it'd upset all those old grannies and their snotty two-faced church. Trouble is, that vicar never left, so I didn't get the chance.'

I wasn't sure where this was leading, but the poor boy was traumatised in some way. Even Debbie must have seen it, as she had stopped her sniping.

'Go on, Sean. There's more than that, isn't there?'

He nodded. 'They've been doing work at the church. You know, renovations? Rewiring it and stuff. There were a load of cables lying at the back of the church when I was in there. By the cabinets with all the skulls and stuff. Didn't think anything of it at the time. Anyway, I needed a crib for a couple of days, and I knew Miss Castle was usually away weekends, so thought I'd chance my luck on this place. I found that window open up there.' He vaguely pointed in the direction of a small window fifteen feet up, which was closed but not latched shut. This was where he had made his entrance a few minutes earlier, shimmying down a wooden post to the floor. 'It was easy enough to climb up the outside of the house and let myself in. I figured, stay here for a couple of nights and then move on. She'd probably never know I'd been here, you dig?'

'But you got more than you bargained for, didn't you?' I coaxed, starting to realise what had happened.

Sean nodded. 'I went around the house exploring, and that's when I saw her, just hanging there. The chair had been kicked away and it was lying on the floor. I'll never forget what she looked like. It was horrible.'

'I'm sure it was, loon,' I said, and put a soothing hand on his arm. He smiled back at me appreciatively, and wiped away a tear with his leather sleeve.

'But the cable in the church,' he continued. 'It was that cloth covered wire. You don't see it much. I think maybe it's probably a bit old-fashioned, yeah? It's the same stuff Miss Castle used to hang herself.'

I glanced over at Debbie, who stared at Sean intently. He still didn't meet her gaze or mine, hiding behind a curtain of shaggy long hair.

'You swear you didn't kill Veronica yourself?' she asked.

He looked up at her, a wild horror, just a heartbeat away from panic in his young eyes. 'No way. I would never do that to someone. Especially not a lady. I mean, I'll bean their house or car, but that's it. I'd never actually hurt anyone.'

A Jubilee Murder

'It's okay, Sean. We believe you,' I said reassuringly, and gave Debbie a quick wink. 'So, you waited for the police and ambulance and reporters to go, and have been biding here all weekend. Don't you think your parents might be fretting a wee bit?'

'They never did before. Don't see why they should start now.'

I turned to Debbie. 'What do you think we should do now, hen?'

She shrugged. 'We should call the police and tell them we've solved one of their crimes for them.'

Sean nodded unhappily, and made no effort to protest.

'I'm not sure,' I pondered. 'It'll be tricky to explain why we're in here.'

'Why *are* you here?' he asked.

'Investigating Veronica's – Miss Castle's – death. We're not sure it was a suicide, and that someone else might have been responsible.' I pondered the situation for a moment as I crouched there, watching the unhappy boy-man. 'You're going to have to go home, Sean. You're going to have to go home and talk to your parents. If you cannae work it out with them, you'll have to leave and set up somewhere else. But one thing's for sure: you have to stop going around attacking people's houses with baked beans.'

He sniggered ruefully. 'Yeah, you're right. I can dig that. You're not going to call the police, then?'

I glanced up at Debbie who just shrugged in an "it's

up to you" gesture.

'No, I don't think so. No police. But if we hear of any more baked bean attacks, we're sending them straight to your door, you hear me?'

He nodded emphatically and heaved his spindly body upright. 'Thanks. No more beans. I promise.'

'Don't go forgetting your duffel bag. You may get hungry on the way home,' I teased, nodding at the holdall on the sofa. 'And maybe go out the back door this time, and not the window?'

He sniffed the last of his tears away and grinned in a very boyish manner.

Once he was gone, I turned to Debbie.

'You are such a soft touch,' she grinned. 'Anyway, what do we do now? We can prove that Veronica didn't kill herself. What's next?'

'We may know she didn't kill herself, but are still no closer to finding out who did. I'll call Colin in the morning, although with jubilee celebrations going on everywhere, I'd doubt anybody will be too bothered about this until long after the public events are over.'

'Well, I don't think Veronica's going anywhere just yet.'

We spent the next twenty minutes fruitlessly hunting for Veronica's last will and testament, or anything that might give some clue as to who might have wanted her dead, but there didn't seem to be anything. At least, there was nothing obvious in drawers or cupboards, bedside cabinets or folders. It would have been nice if I could have not only been able to tell Constable Cropper that Veronica had indeed been killed unlawfully, but also give him a clue as to who was responsible. However, we finally conceded that this was not to be.

'Time to give it up, quine,' I eventually said, hearing the weariness in my voice.

'I think you're right. I'm not getting any less nervous creeping about in this house. Now you have a promise to keep.'

'I do?'

'I was assured there would be cake. Time for you to honour your end of the bargain.'

So it was.

By the time we got back to Frisky Pigeons, it was nearly eleven o' clock. Predictably, Fergus was still awake and earnestly reading that literary masterpiece, Android Planet. From the speed he was getting through it, the novel must have been quite riveting.

'Tea okay for you, Debs?' I asked as I grabbed the kettle and started to fill it.

'Fine. Tea goes better with chocolate cake than potato wine.'

'You know the cake's not finished yet, aye? It still needs a chocolate coating and decoration.'

'I know, I know, but you need someone impartial to judge it for you. Just imagine if you got there tomorrow and they tried your cake, and it turned out to be rank. "Acclaimed Baking Judge is a Fraud!" the headline would read. "Charlatan! Charlatan!", they would cry.'

A Three Villages Mystery

'Don't!' I pleaded, holding up a hand to stem the assault. The worst thing was that there was a small kernel of truth to that. 'Okay, just as long as you know, so no judging an unfinished cake.' While the kettle boiled, I started heating a pan of water and began breaking chocolate into a bowl for melting. The two cakes were properly set now and looked good enough to eat as they were, but I knew this was only half the experience. 'The recipe's designed for the sweetness of the chocolate to balance the slight bitter saltiness of the inside, so it may not be—'

'Oh never mind your baking mumbo jumbo, just give me cake!'

'All right, all right,' I chuckled, and carved a slice for her and popped it on a fawn side plate with geometric flowery patterns around the edge.

'Fork?' I offered.

'Uh-uh. Fingers were made before forks,' she replied, picking up the slice and staring at it with almost covetous desire. She took a bite, her other hand coming up to catch the crumbs.

'Well?' I asked. 'Does it get the Debbie Dugdale seal of approval?'

'Hmm… Could be a bit sweeter,' she replied. Actually, the reply was more along the lines of, "Hwoob wee hweefwer", but I got the gist.

'Which is why I said it needs the chocolate coating!' Honestly, talking to Debbie was like talking to a ten-year-old sometimes, and I already had one of those.

'Wup waywickwy wewiphwus,' came the completely incoherent response.

'Fit you say?'

'I said, basically delicious, you deaf mare.' She waved me away, wanting to be left alone with her cake.

I slid a frosted glass mug of tea over to her. She needed something wet and warm to wash the cake down with. Then it was time to start melting the chocolate in the bowl over the warm water.

'You think he was telling the truth?' I asked as I gently stirred lumps of chocolate in the bowl.

'I'm not sure he's telling the whole truth, but if you're asking whether I think Sean killed Veronica? No, absolutely not. If he'd wanted to, he'd have smashed her over the head and at best, dumped her body in a ditch. I can't see him going to the trouble of staging a suicide.'

'Me neither. I think I just needed to hear it from you.'

Debbie took a sip of her tea and pulled a face. 'Ugh, tastes well bitter after that cake.'

'I'm not surprised. Just imagine what it'd be like if you'd bothered to wait until the chocolate was on top, instead of being a greedy pig and having it early.'

'Early? It's nearly half past eleven. Speaking of which, I guess I should be getting back to his nibs and Lucifer's henchmen.'

'You really are a model parent.' The chocolate chunks were now leaving a thick, brown film over the bowl as I stirred. The chunks soon forming little bergs in a chocolate soup before they disappeared altogether.

'We still don't know who it was, though,' Debbie sighed. 'I'm just not sure we're going to work it out.'

'We will. I just canna help thinking that the key to all this lies in the past, and that begs the question: was Jack Wimble involved?'

'But I thought you said earlier that if he was going to kill her, he would've done it two years ago.'

'I didn't say he did it. I said "involved".' With all the chocolate melted, I took the bowl and placed it on the counter, poured in the rest of the chocolate, and started stirring it.

'So he may know who it was, or perhaps he was controlling someone else?'

'Exactly. And that makes me think of the tractor driver.'

'Barry Huckstep.'

'Or Terry Willes. Maybe one of the older Willes sons.'

'Or half the village,' Debbie grumbled, emitting a low growl of frustration.

I kept stirring the chocolate as it gradually cooled, taking out some of my own frustration on the thickening goo. 'Listen,' I said, 'I'm going to talk to Col— to Constable Cropper tomorrow. I'll tell him what we've learned.'

'Which isn't that much, when you come to think of it.'

'It'll be enough; you'll see. Then it'll be out of our hands. The police will begin a proper investigation and with a bit of luck and a following wind, they'll catch him. Whoever "him" is.'

'You're right,' Debbie sighed, taking a last gulp of tea and dragging her weary body to her feet. 'Now I do need to get going. I'll see you at the jubilee tomorrow?'

'You'd better. I don't want to go judging the jubilee cake mafia without you there as my backup. Can you let yourself out?'

'I don't know. Depends on your cranky front door. If I'm back in five minutes, you'll know I didn't make it. Catch you on the flip side,' she said with an offhand wave, and was gone.

A few seconds later I heard the rattling and repeated slamming of the front door, which clattered in its frame one last time, and she was gone. A sudden, welcome peace descended on Frisky Pigeons.

It was going to be a late night. I still had one and seven eighths of a cake to complete, and a Doctor Who costume to finish putting together.

Oh well, I thought as I put the bowl back on the pan. Sleep was for wimps.

Seventeen

One of these days, I was sure, I would take a large, hefty hammer to my alarm clock. I hated it with a passion. In fact, my hatred for it rivalled my hatred of fennel, and I really, really hated that.

My listless hand flapped around the top of the bedside cabinet, nudging a glass of water and sending my half read copy of Mrs Dalloway tumbling to the floor, the bookmark fluttering down in its wake. My fingers eventually found the alarm clock, a loathsome little box of misery around the same size as the Virginia Woolf novel, with a "simulated wood cabinet". That was what had sold it. Nothing says classy like a brown plastic box.

My fingers eventually found the snooze button and the soul-jarring beeps were mercifully silenced. I prized open one recalcitrant eyelid and peered at the flip numbers on the clock, vision too blurry at first to even make out my own hand clearly, but after several seconds of repeated blinking there was a brief moment of clarity. Seven o' clock, which changed to a minute past as I watched.

I did so hate that clock.

A few minutes later I had dragged my body from the bed and was in the shower, trying to wake myself up first with cool water (which I rapidly concluded was an appalling idea) and then with hot. For a wonder, it sort of worked. My brain, which was not all that razor sharp at the best of times, began to wrench itself into gear. I could almost hear the rusty cogs squeaking as they began to turn.

For some reason, my mind had been fixed on a singular notion: that Veronica had been hanged in her own house. I had thought that someone had accompanied her home from the church, and murdered her there, somehow convincing her to put her head in a noose without struggling. "No defensive marks", Colin had told me. How did you hang someone without them struggling? Tie her up first and then hang her? No, surely the ropes would leave marks on her wrists. Knock her out? No, again, there would be physical evidence. Drugs maybe? They would show up in a toxicology report. Conclusion: she could not have been hanged.

The realisation hit me like some physical force and my knees went slightly weak. I leaned against the wall of the shower, allowing it to steady me. We'd been looking at this all wrong. She wasn't hanged; she was strangled. Strangled with a length of the same cable that had been used in St Luke's church. In fact (I was on fire this morning) she may not have been killed in the house at all.

It could have happened in the church. Now that I came to think about it, she had almost certainly died there. She had gone to the church, been killed there and her body taken back to the house. How had they gotten in, though? *Because she had a key on her, you numptie!* So I was not quite on fire, but definitely a little singed around the edges.

I was about as clean as I was going to get today, so turned the shower off and stepped out, grabbing a large towel and rubbing my head like I was sandpapering an old piece of furniture. Fabric softener, I thought. I wanted nice fluffy towels, not something that would take off the top six layers of my epidermis.

When I was dry enough, albeit exfoliated to the point of glowing an angry shade of cranberry, I slung on my dressing gown. It was while I was brushing my teeth that I started to think of various ways that Veronica could have been strangled. The lack of injuries, other than those around her neck, was a problem. I tried to imagine the situation. Did someone sneak up from behind, the length of cable wrapped several times around their wrists? Did she know the person was there, but did nothing and didn't even turn around to look at them? How would that work? A lover, I mused. What if a lover was behind, maybe kissing her neck, putting her at her ease? She wouldn't expect him to attack her.

I tried to imagine it, the way the cord would suddenly appear and wrap around her throat and constrict. My head jerked back, my hands instinctively snapping up to grab the cable. Fingernails could well break as they clawed at the wire, scratching the skin on my neck. Veronica didn't have any such marks. Why? If her hands weren't tied, then what? Maybe her hands weren't, but her arms might have been. Would the police have checked her arms? Probably. It would have been a huge mistake to miss anything like that. Colin had also said that she had been seen by a pathologist as well. One person might have missed such marks, but two surely couldn't. Was it possible there *were* marks, but they had dismissed them as unrelated?

Tap, tap, tap, came a knock at the bathroom door.

'Mum, you going to be long?' came a tired little voice. 'I really need a wee-wee.'

'I'll just be a minute,' I yelled back, and finished cleaning my teeth.

I was preoccupied as I knocked up some scrambled eggs on toast for my young lord and master. I didn't normally do him a cooked breakfast on a weekday, but this wasn't any ordinary Monday. This was the big jubilee day. We would both need something substantial to fortify our systems.

Once he was settled down at the table and tucking in, his eyes glued to the Six Million Dollar Man comic strip in the latest issue of Look-in, I left him to it and went out to the hall to call my friendly policeman. I flicked through the phone book again, remembering this time that, miraculously, a policeman might be listed under "P", and dialled the number. A few seconds later, it was answered.

'Good morning, Swanhurst Police. Can I help you?' The telephonist sounded a little less irked than her colleague from the other evening. Her voice was younger, with a hint of life and vitality still apparent.

'Hi. Would it be possible to speak to Constable Colin Cropper?' I should have just tape recorded my conversation from the other night.

'Er, I'll put you through to his desk. It should just be a sec.'

The line went dead for a few seconds, and I was beginning to wonder whether she had cut me off completely, but then I heard another ringing tone. A good ten seconds went by before the phone was answered.

'Hiya, Colin?'

'Sorry, Constable Cropper isn't available right now,' a fresh female voice said in a sing-song, but oddly vacant tone. 'This is WPC Walraven. Can I help, or take a message?'

'Oh, hi,' I replied, slightly taken aback and cursing my familiarity. It had never occurred to me that someone else might answer his phone. Eejit. 'No, I was hoping to speak to Constable Cropper about… an ongoing issue. My name's Catriona Cameron. Do you think—'

'Oh, hello,' she interrupted in an overtly friendly manner. 'He's told us all about you.'

'He has?'

'Yes, but he never mentioned you were Scottish. How interesting.'

'Is it?' I replied, completely befuddled and not sure how this conversation worked. 'Anyway, perhaps you could give him a message for me.'

'Actually, he's left a message for *you*. He said it's on the off chance that you might call.'

'Me in particular, or anybody in general?'

'No, you in particular. Catri-o-na Cameron.' She made a point of over-pronouncing the silent "o" in Catriona. 'Let me see if I can find it, duck. Ah, here it is. He says he's doing traffic liaison work this morning, but he should be at the Downscliffe Jubilee Party sometime after one o' clock this afternoon, should you – and he's put this quite specifically – "want to stop by for a chat".'

I wasn't sure what to make of that. Did he have some more information on the case? If so, I needed to speak with him as soon as. Unless he meant something else? No, couldn't be that.

'Okay,' I said, 'thank you so much for your help. I take it he didn't say anything else?'

'Anything else, duck? About what in particular?'

'Oh, nothing. Doesn't matter. Goodbye, and thanks again.'

I dropped the telephone receiver lightly back onto its cradle. I really wasn't very good at playing this game, and wasn't even sure what this game was in the first place. And why was this WPC calling me "duck". Oh well, it'd all come out in the wash. I still had an awful lot to learn about living in the south of England.

Fergus came sauntering past, his face still buried in

his magazine. He didn't seem to have much interest in the articles on Showaddywaddy or Berni Flint, but was now avidly reading The Tomorrow People comic strip.

'Your costume's on your bed,' I said, and he stopped abruptly, a big grin erupting on his face, and tore through to his room to study it. A few seconds later, I heard an appreciative "groovy", and the rustling of fabric. Somehow, one word of appreciation like that made all those hours of work and lack of sleep worthwhile.

I popped into the pantry to check on the cake. I wasn't sure what might have happened to it overnight, but felt happier taking another peek at it, just in case. It was inside a big beige Tupperware box, which was upside down so the lid formed the base. As gently as I could, because no one was more aware than me of what a klutz I could be, I prized it open. There was an immediate, overwhelming blast of pure chocolate, an aroma that gave me an almost lightheaded euphoria, just for a moment. The cake looked fine, the chocolate coating rich and shiny, covered with thick white and dark chocolate shavings. Around the edges were half a dozen dollops of piped cream, each topped with a glacé cherry. The decorations weren't strictly necessary, but just made it a little more appealing. The first bite is with the eye and all that.

The other cake – the one with the missing slice courtesy of Mrs Deborah Dugdale – was in another box, this one in garish orange. I thought it would be a good idea, or maybe even my duty, to cut a slice for myself, just to make sure it was okay. That was my excuse, and I didn't really care that I was eating chocolate cake at half past nine in the morning.

I was just raising the slice of confectionery heaven to my mouth when, of course, the phone rang. It was Debbie, and I immediately heard the sound of Freddie and Arthur, her two ten-year-old boys, playing in the background.

'Hey there, foxy mama. What's the buzz?' she asked, the noise in the background getting louder. 'Will you two horrid little monsters just shut up? Can't hear myself think!'

I had to stifle a giggle, my mind painting a picture of the scene at the other end of the phone. 'Having a fun morning, Debs?'

'Is infanticide still a crime in this country?'

'I'm afraid it is.'

'Kids, pack your bags. We're moving to Cambodia or Lebanon or somewhere else that you won't be missed!'

This threat didn't seem to have an appreciable effect for more than a few seconds, the screaming and whooping resuming with renewed gusto. I was starting to appreciate why Debbie liked to spend so much time at my house.

'I'm just getting things together for today. In fact, I was about half a second away from trying this cake when you so rudely – I mean, so graciously – decided to enrich my life with a telephone call.'

'I'll keep it brief, then. Hate to keep a woman from her cake.'

A Three Villages Mystery

'People have been murdered for less.'

'Take a chill pill, sister. What time you heading on down?'

'We're setting off at ten-thirty. Fergs is just trying on his costume. If he likes it, I dare say I'll have to prize it off him come tonight.'

'Cool. We'll do the same. Looks like we'll have ourselves a li'l old convoy on the way down to the village hall. Check ya later.'

There was something about talking to Debbie that sometimes left me feeling that a tornado had just torn through the house.

I went back into the pantry and was reunited with my slice of cake. Now that the phone call with Debbie was out of the way, I was free to have some quality time with it.

'Mum?'

It's a conspiracy, I thought. 'Which would you prefer: Cambodia or Lebanon?'

'Eh?'

'Never mind. What is it?'

A miniature Tom Baker appeared at the doorway to the pantry, and for a moment – admittedly a very brief moment – I forgot my cake. He looked fantastic. Just a cute little miniature version of the real thing.

'Wow, you look braw, loon,' I exclaimed, unable to hide the grin on my face, even if I'd wanted to. 'Are you happy with it?'

'It's off the hook, Mum!' he beamed back, flicking a

lock of smelly wig away from his face.

The two scarf idea had worked a charm, the two ends trailing on the floor. I wondered if I would be able to keep count of the number of times he tripped over it today. He had, after all, drawn the short straw in life and inherited his mother's clumsiness.

'Oh, one last thing,' I said, turning back toward the shelves in the pantry. 'Now where did I put it?' I mused as I scanned the room, tapping an index finger against my lips. 'Ah, there it is,' I said with some relief, retrieving a small white paper bag.

'What is it?'

'A bag of jelly babies, just to complete the ensemble.'

He grinned, and tucked the bag away in his pocket.

'Gimme some skin, bro,' I said, holding my hand out for a low five. He reciprocated and we smacked palms. 'Now be gone with you, child, and leave me alone with my cake.'

The little mound of long coat and scarf and floppy hat scurried off and disappeared into his room. Finally, I could have some uninterrupted cake time.

I wasn't disappointed.

Eighteen

ownscliffe had probably not seen this much frivolity and public exuberance since the Coronation itself. Bunting criss-crossed the roads, flags hung limply from windows and chimneys. Children ran along the pavements, waving miniature Union Flags and screaming happily. Along Old School Lane, a low-key street party had been set up, the little road closed for the day. Flimsy collapsible tables had been set up and were piled high with tubs of sandwiches, pasties, sausages, cheese and pineapple on sticks, Victoria sponge cakes with jam oozing from the centres and lavish bowls of trifle. Even out on Ashfield Lane, we could hear brass band music playing through tortured speakers, along with the boom-boom-boom of a bass drum.

It was a windy day and there had been a little rain overnight. I could envisage the members of the Jubilee Celebration Committee waking up this morning, nervously peeking out of their windows, and sagging with relief when they saw the last of the grey clouds evaporating and blue skies taking their place. The only clouds around now were white and fluffy, and not at all threatening as they scudded across the sky.

Outside The Blue Bell, three extravagantly decorated floats were waiting to make their ponderous journey through the village, imitation Coldstream Guards wearing black fluffy tea cosies were loitering around the flatbed trailers, several of them trying their luck and chatting up Her Majesty Queen Elizabeth II, who herself was nursing half a pint of cider and giggling at the attention. Prince Charles was also there, sporting a pair of comedy ears and already looking slightly the worse for wear.

Once they had completed their tour of the village, the floats and their passengers – those who had not fallen off on the way – would arrive at the playing field behind the school and the village hall. This was where most of the spectators had already gathered, ready to wave and cheer to "Her Majesty" when she arrived. The field was a riot of red, white and blue, mixed with a smattering of marquees, fun fare games and vintage cars.

When our little convoy – all two cars of us – arrived at the village hall, its modest car park was completely full, however Jack Wimble owned the field next door and the overflow was permitted to use that. It was sheer good fortune that the weather had been mostly dry over the past couple of days, notwithstanding the overnight showers, otherwise the farmer would be towing the cars out again in a scene less like the Coronation, and more like the

Battle of the Somme. The field itself was quite rough, and Ernie's soft suspension meant we were wobbling back and forth like Oliver Reed let loose in a Highland distillery. I parked up in the nearest space I could find, not wishing to invite a bout of seasickness on today of all days. Even this corner of the field was beginning to fill up, and the crew of the St John's Ambulance were gesticulating to newcomers not to block them in. A moment later, Debbie's Hillman Avenger, complete with two bouncy disciples of Satan in the back, pulled up next to us. Her car was a fancy-shmancy four-door saloon, and as soon as the vehicle had come to a halt, a diminutive Laurel and Hardy had the back doors open and were tearing around like a pair of demented Homepride flour men, their bowler hats bouncing around completely independent of their heads.

'Shut up, you horrible children!' I heard Debbie yell as she was getting out of the car. 'Wotcha foxy,' she shouted when she saw me emerge from Ernie. 'How's it hangin'?'

'Hey there, Debs,' I yelled back as I set my sunglasses firmly in place. I was determined not to have any ACHOO syndrome incidents today.

She gave me a swift appraisal, and a wink. 'Looking stellar, doll.'

She always did this to me, and I was never sure whether she was just being kind and generous, or if she really enjoyed making me feel uncomfortable and self-conscious. I suspected it was the latter, although I had at least gone to a little effort today. I was wearing a summer frock, with a marigold and pansy pattern, the hem just brushing my calves and the sleeves wafting loosely around my elbows. Honestly, I looked like a giant fruit salad with a gingernut garnish. It wasn't too extravagant, and certainly not enough to attract any undue attention, but I thought it would be appropriate for a well-dressed baking contest judge. Not to mention the fact that there might well be a photographer from the Mercury here today, and I didn't want to look like a complete dogs' dinner if I happened to end up in the paper.

The fact that I was also expecting to see a certain member of Her Majesty's Constabulary had absolutely nothing to do with it. Nothing whatsoever.

Debbie's hands came up to cover her mouth when she saw Fergus emerge from the car. 'Oh he looks completely adorable!' she cried, and I wasn't about to disagree, although I might have been just a tad biased.

Fergus loathed being called cute or adorable or any similar appellations, and turned his lip up in a disgruntled sneer. His disgust was short-lived though, and he went running after his friends. We watched with delighted attention as Laurel and Hardy went tearing off after a yelling, laughing Doctor Who, his scarf billowing behind him.

There was a screaming whine from the PA system, and not a face in the field failed to wince. The master of ceremonies was about to speak.

'My Lords, Ladies and gentlemen, may I 'ave your

attention, if you please?'

I turned to Debbie and whispered in her ear, 'It's Parker! It's Parker from Thunderbirds.'

She made no attempt to disguise her laughter, and let out a cackle that rivalled the volume of the speakers.

'I am pleased to be able to inform you that 'Er Majesty Queen Elizabeth the Second, Defender of the Faith, Empress of India and all that, will be joinin' us shortly. I want you all to give 'er a big royal wave an' an even bigger royal cheer when she appears. Would yourselves like to 'ave a little practice, so to speak? One, two… Wait for it, you at the back… Three.'

Most of the crowd joined in, and let out a raucous round of applause. Debbie and I were just about the only ones not cheering, because we were too busy holding onto each other as we laughed and tried not to wee ourselves.

'I'm afraid I can't 'ear you. Shall we try that again, ladies and gentlemen? A one, a two, a three.'

An even bigger roar erupted from the crowd, who had been whipped into an almost delirious frenzy. Our friend, the MC, may have been an inadvertently funny little man, but he sure knew how to get a crowd going.

'Oh, that's much better. I think I can 'ear 'Er Majesty approaching right now, so get ready to give 'er a good old British welcome when she, you know, turns up.'

'Oh, he's priceless, ain't he?' Debbie shouted over the shouts of the crowd.

'Move over Terry Wogan,' I yelled back, 'Parker from Downscliffe is taking over.'

A Jubilee Murder

Over the noise from the jubilant jubilee crowd, I heard the sound of air horns approaching, like a discordant musical symphony where none of the musicians knew what the others were playing.

The first of the floats hove into view, followed by the second and the third. I hoped they weren't going to make Her Majesty park in the next field as we had. I could just imagine her being tossed unceremoniously headfirst into a cow pat. But no, space had been allotted for the three lorries in the playing field. The floats trundled through and took up their positions next to the handful of marquees and tents erected in the area.

Prince Charles was the first to leap off his float, stumbling and landing on his hands and knees with giant ears flapping back and forth like the wings of a demented seagull. He immediately leapt up again and spread his arms wide in triumph. I wondered whether the Queen had abdicated and this parody not-so-bonny Prince Charlie here had acceded to the throne instead.

'What a vulgar performance,' I heard a voice behind me exclaim. It was a voice I recognised and I groaned.

'Mrs Popplewell,' I said, plastering on a smile that was as phony as our own Prince of Wales's plastic ears. 'I do agree. Absolutely shocking.' She wore a huge, flowing caftan dress in what looked like railway green. And when I say huge, it was absolutely colossal. I was pretty sure a camping shop could sell it as a four-berth tent once she was done with it. I just hoped there wouldn't be a freak gust of wind or we'd all be needing therapy come the end of the day. This was disturbingly likely with it being so blustery.

'Oh, hello Catriona, dear. And this is your little friend, isn't it?' she crowed, casting an eye in Debbie's direction. "Little" friend was pushing it a bit. She had a good two inches on me.

Debbie gave a little curtsey. 'Ooh, it's Debbie, Miss. Caty's bestest friend, Miss. Awfully good to see you again, Miss.'

There were times I could kiss Debbie, and other times I could murder her. I wasn't sure which category this episode fell into.

'I'll be judging the baking contest later,' I butted in, before Debbie could get me into real trouble. 'In fact, I've made a cake of my own, just to prove that I can. I would've felt like a bit of a fraud otherwise.'

Mrs Popplewell looked taken aback. 'I'm sure nobody would have thought that, my dear. It was very good of you to step in at the last moment.'

'Thank you.'

'And I'm sure everyone will make allowances for your amateurishness, under the circumstances.'

Well wasn't that just lovely. I wondered if there was any more of that electrical cable around for me to throttle her with.

'Catriona,' came another voice, and I saw Maureen from the shop bustling toward me, apologising to people she bumped into. She wore a blue and white gingham dress that may have been fashionable fifteen years earlier, although I doubted it. The dress may not have seen the light of day for a decade or two, but she still wore her comfy old Hush Puppies. It took my plodding brain a second to equate her face with an identity. I wasn't sure that I had ever seen her out of her shop clothes. 'Oh, it's such a relief to see you. I had visions of you not turning up.'

'Nonsense. I made a royal cake of my own, just to prove to myself I could do it.'

'Young Catriona here thought we might think her a fraud,' Mrs Popplewell explained for me. 'I told her she was just being silly. We have every confidence in her, don't we Mrs Bishop?'

Maureen agreed, with a fervent nod of the head. 'Absolutely. We were lucky you agreed to help us. In fact, if all goes well, I can see this becoming a regular event.'

'I'm not sure we can arrange jubilees all that often,' I pointed out, quite deadpan in my delivery. It took a few moments, but Maureen eventually cottoned on, emitting a squeak of laughter, and giving me a playful shove on the shoulder.

'Oh, you are a one, Catriona. I wish I could be so funny.' She continued to chuckle, and I wondered if it was completely genuine, and soon concluded that it was. Now I was worried about her mental stability.

'Yes, yes, I think that's enough, Mrs Bishop,' Mrs Popplewell said sternly. She clearly did not appreciate my comedic efforts. 'Perhaps you could begin setting up in the royal bakery contest marquee.'

A Three Villages Mystery

'Of course,' Maureen said, feeling suitably chastised. 'Catriona, would you be very kind and bring your own cake? I'm now dying to show the other gals what you've done.'

Just before I turned back to the car, I saw Her Majesty waving regally to the crowd, a swarm of young girls around her watching with rapt attention. This was the nearest most had come to a real queen, albeit a real queen who was hiding half a glass of cider under the folds of her royal gown. As musical accompaniment, the brass band music fired up again, half deafening anyone who had foolishly strayed too close to the large metal speakers that looked as though they had been in service when George V had been on the throne.

It was with a little anxiety that I opened the cake box to peer inside, but it had not shifted on the way here from Frisky Pigeons, and the increasing heat had not yet had an adverse effect. Now I just had to get past Mrs Popplewell's discriminating eye, which would be a minor miracle.

Leaning in to retrieve the cake box from the back of the car was not my most dignified position, but the cake's welfare was the main priority and it needed protecting over anything else. Almost anything. As I straightened up, I caught sight of a diminutive time lord hairing around the busy field, still being chased by a maniacal Laurel and Hardy. I didn't have a hand free, so bumped the car door closed with my backside and, predictably, my frock got caught. Typical. I could wear a dress 365 days a year, and would guarantee that the only time – the *only* time – that it got caught was when I didn't have a hand free.

'What would you do without me?' Debbie asked, opening the car door and setting me free.

'Thanks Debs,' I said with a grin. I was under no illusions; I knew full well how dopey I could be, as I'd just demonstrated. In the playing field, the hordes of people parted for a second and I caught a glimpse of Doctor Who, his big floppy hat having been replaced by a black bowler. He now looked like a miniature bohemian bank manager.

'I swear they got swapped at the maternity hospital,' Debbie groaned as she watched the boys. 'They're certainly not mine.'

We set off in the direction of a moderately-sized fabric structure, the other side of the main marquee. Overhead, strings of bunting were whipped by the wind, fluttering wildly. We strolled through a collection of classic cars: Austin Cambridges, MGAs and Austin Healey 3000s, Morris Minors, A Triumph TR2, and even a Messerschmitt bubble car, that I happened to know belonged to Celia Fernsby-Brown's long suffering and terminally hen-pecked husband. It had been pushed here from the church that morning, being about as reliable as a Met Office weather forecast. I think the cars were all supposed to be from around the time of the Coronation, but there seemed to be quite a bit of leeway here.

'They don't seem to take after Tony, that's for sure,' I said as we passed a trio of Citroën 2CVs and one dented and rusty Citroën Diane, the four French cars seeming to be huddling together for mutual protection. 'Speaking of which, where is the big guy?'

Her eyes rolled heavenward. 'How about I give you three guesses, but I'd wager you'd only need one?'

'Oh no, he's not working *again*, is he? Does that loon ever take a break?'

'It's "all for us" he tells me. He's "building a future" for us all. Right now, I'd settle for a present and let the future take care of itself.'

I sympathised with her, but could also understand his position. I was lucky that my job was about as flexible as they came, so I could spend as much time with Fergus as he or I pleased.

We arrived at the baking marquee and I was about to duck behind the entrance flap when I saw a lone figure plodding past. He was old and white-haired, wearing well-worn corduroy trousers in a shiny dark mustard colour. His burgundy jumper was equally venerable, with numerous holes and loose threads hanging down.

'Is that Wally Moore?' I asked, and Debbie followed where I was looking. I couldn't very well point, with a large cake box in my arms that I cradled like a long lost lover.

'Yeah, I think it is. He's going into… Is that The Old Badger or The Blue Bell tent?'

Both of the village pubs were represented here today, and plastic glasses were already littering the benches and the grass. 'It's The Old Badger tent. Look, there's Gemma serving drinks. Dotty must be back at the pub. This would be a perfect time, though.'

'Perfect time for what?'

'To go speak to Wally. I can ply him with alcohol and see what he can tell me. I'm sure he has a story he wants to tell. He's been keeping quiet about Veronica for all these years. Surely he would be willing to speak now?'

'I wouldn't bet on it, but knock yourself out. Just don't be a bunny; we don't know for sure whether he killed her himself yet. He might happily bump you off to keep you quiet. You catch my drift?'

Now there was a cheery thought. 'I knew I kept you around for a reason. Always there to calm my nerves. Do me a solid, would you?'

She shrugged.

'Dump this cake in the tent, and then keep an eye on Fergus for me.'

'Ten-four, sister. Check you later.'

Nineteen

popped my head around the flap of the drinks tent. It was busy, as I had expected. The clientele appeared to be mostly men escaping the festivities, their wives and children, or just life itself. There were a few couples, whom I had regularly seen together in The Old Badger. I didn't see any other unaccompanied women, though.

I wasn't sure it was the greatest idea I had ever had, coming in here alone, but it was a little late now. I lifted my sunglasses and propped them on my head, half burying them in ginger curls as I weaved my way toward the makeshift bar. This was made up of a couple of rickety trestle tables with a plastic gingham tablecloth slung over the top. Behind these were a dozen or so barrels, lying on their sides and piled atop one another. Plastic glasses were in boxes, stacked to one side and generally getting in the way of the bar staff. I recognised Marianne, and also the ginger-haired girl I'd seen in The Old Badger the other night, as they rushed around trying to keep the punters topped up with life-saving alcohol. Derek was also behind the bar, unhurriedly pouring the odd drink, but spending most of his time chatting amiably to his friends and getting in the way of the two girls. Jack and Kitty Wimble leaned against the bar, the improvised table creaking under her weight. By all accounts, Kitty was quite a stunner in her youth, but had spent too many years indulging a little too readily in the spoils of farm life. She was, by this point, a red cheeked, round faced and equally round bodied woman, happy in herself and quite frankly not giving a damn what anyone else thought. I kind of envied that attitude.

It was warm inside the small marquee. Oppressively warm, with too many bodies crammed together, too much noise of people talking over each other, of others speaking even louder, or raucous laughter from groups of men and punctuated by shrieks and cackles from the women.

Wally Moore stood at the bar, patiently waiting to be served. He was stooped slightly over, his fingers clasped together over his chest as others bustled and jostled around him.

'Hello Wally, I thought it was you,' I shouted above the din of chatter, in as bubbly and friendly a voice as I could muster.

He looked at me in confusion for a moment, until recognition dawned. 'Hello there, young Catriona. May I buy you a drink?'

'Oh, that would be lovely,' I replied, locking my arm in his. 'If they have a dry white wine, I'll have one of those. If not, I'll have anything that's going.' This was the abridged story of my life.

Wally attracted the attention of the ginger-haired girl, who poured him a glass of bitter with a huge frothy head, and a large glass of white wine for me. I took a sip as soon as she set it down. Alas, it was room temperature and a little too sweet for my taste, but it was better than nothing.

'Shall we go and sit outside?' I yelled. 'Can't hear myself think in here.'

'Right you are, my dear. That suits me down to the ground, I am thinking.'

We found a bench just beyond the doorway and collapsed onto it. It was one of those where if too much weight is placed on one side, you're likely to go over backwards and end up wearing your drink and have a park bench on top of you. My dignity was a somewhat tenuous concept at the best of times, so a bench-related incident was probably best avoided.

It wasn't quite as noisy and busy outside, but was still a madhouse compared to how the village usually was. The delicate sensibilities of the locals seemed to have been put on hold for the duration of the jubilee. Except for the likes of Mrs Popplewell. I was sure nothing short of a royal decree would force her to crack a smile.

Wally and I said nothing for a while, merely watching the antics of the village as the people enjoyed themselves, all to the beat of a booming bass drum and occasional commentary by the comedy master of ceremonies. I caught a glimpse of Debbie, trying to herd three little boys around and having about as much success as if she'd been trying to herd goldfish.

Men were furiously hurling solid wooden balls in the coconut shy, and apparently having very little success. The coconuts sat atop iron poles, the tops fashioned into hoops, but I had a sneaking suspicion that coconuts and hoops had been hammered together so that nothing short of a cannon shell would shift them. Or they were simply glued in place. Others played on the tombolas and shooting ranges. I spied another stall as well, this one providing freshly-made lemonade. Behind it were half a dozen buckets of ripe, juicy lemons, waiting to be squeezed in a fearsome looking contraption. At the bottom of the field was a small track where a couple of go-karts raced around, while a long queue of eager youngsters watched. Children ran this way and that, some dragging balloons behind them, others burying their faces in candy floss on sticks.

Parents were attempting to gather them up as it was nearly time for commemorative mugs to be distributed in the main marquee. The Jubilee Celebration Committee had taken note of every child in the parish beforehand, and these prized mugs would be given out in alphabetical order. With the surnames of Cameron and Dugdale, Fergus and the twins had good reason to feel smug, although I did pity their other friend, Billy Yates.

'They're all heading off to get their freebies,' Wally muttered. 'Future heirlooms to commemorate this auspicious day.'

A Three Villages Mystery

'You don't sound like you approve?'

'Well, I hardly think this is what Her Majesty had in mind to celebrate twenty-five years on the throne.'

'I think Her Majesty would appreciate so many people going to so much trouble, don't you? I don't think there's a single town or village up or down the country that isn't celebrating today.'

'It's just an excuse though, innit? I mean people get an extra bank holiday today and a free event where they can get drunk and embarrass themselves. That's why they're here; not to honour our reigning monarch.'

He was a barrel of laughs today. Time to shift the conversation in another direction. At least I wouldn't have to worry about dampening his mood. 'I learned something the other day. At least, I heard a rumour.'

'Oh yes?' From his tone, I had the feeling he had an inkling of what was coming.

'You know what I'm going to ask. She was your niece, wasn't she? Bessie Moore.'

He nodded, a rueful look on his face. 'Yes, she was. A wonderful girl, back in the day. Always smiling, always happy. It didn't matter how bad the news was, how dark the future looked, she would always bring a little joy into our lives.'

It was hardly possible to reconcile this description of the young Bessie, with what I knew she would become. The wide-eyed optimism of youth had at some point been swept away, to be replaced by a cynical, hard, almost cruel persona in more recent years. I had been the recipient of some of that venom, and I knew I was not alone in this. I tried to envisage her as an innocent and happy child, bringing joy into people's lives as the Luftwaffe rained flaming terror down from the skies, but the naive figure I imagined bore no resemblance to Veronica Castle.

'But then she grew up, didn't she,' I prodded. 'And that was when Jack Wimble came onto the scene.'

His lips pursed, eyes narrowing as my words sank in. 'Yes, sad day when that happened. Very sad day. Took her childhood from her, he did. She was just a girl, and lost her mind when Jack's eye turned toward her. He was already married to Kitty, did you know that?'

I nodded.

'Didn't matter to him. He took what he wanted and then tossed 'er aside. But he'd ruined her more than he realised. Left her with a burden she could never be free from.'

'The child,' I said. 'I had heard that there was a daughter.'

'That came later, but Jack wanted nothing to do with it. He just wanted rid of young Bessie. It broke her heart. It broke her soul. She was just empty after that.' He took a long swig of his beer, draining the glass almost to the bottom and smacking his lips. 'They wanted her out of the village. They didn't care. They wanted her out. Her, her parents. Me. The lot of us.'

'But you didn't go?'

'No, I was damned if I'd be forced from my home

because of Jack Wimble. I stayed. The rest of the family had to go. Cackett arranged it.'

'The vicar?'

'Oh, he wasn't the vicar at the time. He was best friends with Jack. Thick as thieves, they were. Still are, in some respects. Silas Cackett arranged to have all of us moved away. Said our lives wouldn't be worth living if we stayed. Jack would see to that, he said.'

That explained why the reverend had no problem with Jack Wimble giving the reading at the Sunday service.

'And the daughter?' I asked. 'What happened to her?'

Wally shrugged and finished the last of his beer. 'Cackett dealt with that, too. Had the baby taken away from Bessie and put into care. That was the final thing that broke her. She never wanted to lose that wee nipper, but she wasn't given any choice. They took Bessie's baby, and in so doing they took her heart.'

He twirled the glass around in his fingers for a few moments, staring at the patterns the bubbles had left on its side.

'What happened the other day, Wally? When you found her. Did you see anything?'

'How do you mean?'

'I mean, do you think she killed herself, or do you suspect someone else?'

'You saying she was murdered?' He sat back, considering this for a moment. 'I've thought about this. I've thought about this a lot, and I'm sure there's someone else involved. Bessie didn't kill herself. She'd rebuilt her life. She still held all those memories from before, but she was a big success now, and she was happy. It wasn't just happy for the outside world to see, but she was happy full stop.'

'Then why did she come back? After all those years, why did she come back to the one village where her life had fallen apart before?'

I was surprised to see Wally's face dissolve into a smile. 'She wanted to rub Jack Wimble's nose in it, that's why. She wanted to be a constant reminder to him of what he'd given up. He hated it, but there was nothing he could do about it. She was back, reminding him and reminding Kitty of what he had done all those years ago.'

'But would he kill her, though?' I asked, forming a picture in my head. 'To make it all go away again. I mean, he and the vicar might have tried again to force her to leave, but they had no leverage over her now. Was murder the only way to get rid of her?'

'I wondered about that,' Wally mused. 'I've called Jack Wimble all the names under the sun over the past thirty odd years. I vowed never to set foot in that church because of the role Cackett played. But I can't see them as murderers. I just can't, much as I'd like to.'

'In that case, do you have any idea who might have done it?' I finished the last of my wine.

'Not specifically. I know that she had… friends. Dalliances. She was no angel. I wondered if it was one of her acquaintances. Jack Wimble might not have killed her, but per'aps it were some boyfriend who wanted rid of her, or a jealous wife.'

I couldn't answer. Wally had filled in a few of the gaps in my knowledge, but the truth was still tantalisingly out of my reach. The answer was there, I was sure of it. I just needed a little more.

'Another drink, Wally?' I asked, putting an arm around him in comradeship and squeezing him tight. 'You look like you need it.'

He plonked his glass down in front of me. 'You're a good lass, Catriona, and don't let anyone tell you otherwise.'

'I'll try and remember that next time I talk to Mrs Popplewell,' I grinned.

'Ugh, that old bag.' He shuddered.

There was a commotion behind me, from within the beer tent. It didn't sound like the usual horseplay and tomfoolery that you get at these occasions, even with plenty of alcohol around. Most of the crowd seemed to be gravitating to form a circle around a single point.

One of the younger men – someone I recognised as one of the local farmhands – came rushing out and immediately charged off toward the car park.

'What's happ…' I began, but he was already gone, weaving his way through the throngs of people like a skier on the giant slalom.

Peeking inside, I could see nothing but the backs of people, all staring agog at… something. Sometimes, it was maddening to be five foot five. I had half a mind to leap onto the bar to get a better look, but thought better of it. I wasn't exactly in Kitty Wimble's league, but still didn't trust the ramshackle construction not to collapse. Then the crowd would have two things to gawp at.

'Give him some air,' I heard a voice from within the melee shout, and the circle of onlookers reluctantly shuffled outwards a few feet.

'In here, in here,' another voice shouted, and I turned to see the young farmhand running back, accompanied by two black-uniformed men carrying a stretcher, their distinctive white sashes flapping about as they ran. They muscled their way into the tent, forcing a path through the crowd. The young man stood next to me, his hands on his knees as he tried to catch his breath.

'What happened?' I repeated, hoping that he would stick around long enough this time to answer.

'It's Jack,' he gasped, the pain of the exertion etched onto his face. 'I think he's had a heart attack.'

'Jack Wimble?' I asked, astonished at this news.

He nodded. 'The very same. Keeled over right in front of me, frothing at the mouth and everything. Unless he's got rabies,' he mumbled, suddenly looking quite nervous.

'Frothing at the mouth? Do people normally froth at the mouth with a heart attack?'

'Dunno, love. But he didn't look too clever, I can tell you.'

I felt a hand on my arm, and a very familiar, very welcome voice asked the same question I had. The same question everyone was asking.

'What's happened?' Debbie asked.

'It's Jack Wimble,' I informed her. 'He's had a heart attack. At least, that's what this fellow thinks.' I gestured toward the farmhand, who nodded with enthusiasm.

There was a fresh commotion, and the crowd started to move aside, like Moses parting the Red Sea. The two ambulancemen emerged, carrying the listless figure of a grey-skinned Jack Wimble on the stretcher. His arms dangled from the sides, flapping back and forth languidly. Kitty was fussing over him, tearful and whimpering. There was frothy drool around his mouth, but it was his eyes that really caught my attention. He was just about conscious; it was a bright, sunny day, and yet his pupils were huge black spots, dilated so far that there was barely any iris left visible.

'Did you see his eyes?' Debbie asked, her mouth wide open in shock.

'I did.' I shouted after the ambulancemen. 'Check for poison. Check for belladonna.'

If they heard me, they didn't acknowledge it.

'Bella who?' Debbie enquired, her face twisted into a lopsided frown.

'Deadly nightshade,' I explained. 'One of the effects is dilated pupils. Another effect is profuse frothing at the mouth.'

'You mean he's been poisoned? You're faking me out!'

'No, seriously. I think someone's tried to murder

Jack Wimble.'

I instinctively looked round at Wally Moore, who was still sat serenely at the bench. But now he looked different – a faint hint of a smile was tugging at the corners of his mouth.

Twenty

'Well, I'm no expert but I'd say that rather puts the kibosh on any idea that Jack Wimble was our murderer,' Debbie muttered quietly as we made our way back to the main marquee where the boys were waiting to get their mugs.

It was a testament to good old British cold-hearted stoicism and resolve that within a few minutes, everything had returned to almost normal. The brass band music being piped through the PA system had restarted, there were pings as pop guns were fired and pellets hit the tin wall behind, the thuds of coconuts being clattered by solid wooden projectiles, laughter, singing, frivolity.

'I'm not so sure,' I replied, glancing around me. 'Did you see the look on old Wally Moore's face?'

'Can't say that I did.'

'Well, he wasn't exactly cut up about it, I can tell you. He was actually smiling as the ambulancemen carted Jack Wimble away.'

'So…' Debbie paused as she assimilated this, trying

to form a picture in her mind. 'You reckon he thinks Jack murdered Veronica? Oh my God, that could mean he tried to murder Jack in revenge.'

'Maybe, but we still don't know for sure that it was Jack. Or that today's incident was Wally.'

'I'd say they're both suspects though, wouldn't you?'

'Oh aye, deffo. I wouldn't discount either.' I felt a little shaken by the episode. Until this point, I had thought of Veronica's death as a one-off, that there was no risk to continuing our investigations. But now that certitude had been shattered. Someone had been attacked, and a simple blood test should prove as much as soon as Jack got to the hospital, which meant the police would have to investigate this as a murder. There was no consigning it to a suicide attempt this time.

As we reached the marquee, a little whirlwind came rushing out, scarf waving in the air. He was excitedly brandishing a white mug with a royal crest on the side.

'Mum, Mum, I got it!' Fergus shouted as he barrelled into me. 'Look, isn't it cool?'

He held the mug up for me to examine. I was not sure that in five years' time he would regard a mug with a picture of the Queen on the side as the height of cool, but he was certainly happy enough to get it now.

'Wow, that's fab,' I cried, trying to sound sincere. 'Do you want to give it to me so that it doesn't get broken?'

He thought about this for a second, reasoned that this was probably a wise move, and handed it over. As I tucked it away in my shoulder bag, I caught a glimpse of my watch. Ten past one. Colin should be here by now.

'Where are Stan and Ollie?' I asked.

'Still in there, waiting for their mugs.'

Debbie cast a glance my way. 'I'll just go in and make sure they're okay,' she said, and I could see that she was echoing my own concerns. As much as she complained about her two little horrors, she still thought the world of them and was just as paranoid as I was about something happening to them. I gave her a wink and turned away, guiding Fergus along with me. I wanted to keep him at my side, just for a while.

There was no straight path back up to the village hall, throngs of people wandering, queueing, milling about doing nothing in particular. A line of old women were sat in deck chairs, fanning themselves, sunning themselves, inflicting their varicose veins on innocent bystanders as they dared show their knees in public. It was a crazy modern world we lived in.

I could just make out, parked on the grass at the top of the playing field, the gleaming white bodywork of a motorcycle, surrounded by a gaggle of excited children. Fergus caught one glimpse of the motorbike and he was off, charging the last fifty yards toward it. I stumbled along behind, my Olé chunkies not the most practical thing to wear over the rough ground of the playing field.

When I finally caught up, Fergus was in the thrall of PC Cropper, his eyes glued to the gleaming machine as the constable leant casually against it. I had this sudden worrying notion that Fergus might want to be the next

Barry Sheene. That was pretty much the last thing I wanted him to do. I didn't want him going anywhere near motorbikes.

'Ah, Mrs Cameron,' Constable Cropper said when he saw me. 'Hoping to go for a spin?' He gestured with a flick of his copper-coloured head toward the bike.

'Not on your life,' I said. 'Death traps, these things.'

He didn't seem in the least bit perturbed by my response, and carried on talking to the kids while I looked over the motorcycle dubiously. I had to concede that it was an impressive machine, all shiny, new and freshly polished. For the size of it, he might as well have driven a car. It was huge, with two great saddlebags in white plastic, with a matching oversized fairing at the front and a petrol tank you could practically have a bath in. Perched somewhat incongruously atop this tank was a decidedly old-fashioned black telephone with a coiled wire.

'Have you caught lots of criminals?' asked one of his new fans.

'Thousands,' he replied, and I was surprised to see him give me a wink.

'Wow,' came the response of a dozen enraptured youngsters.

'And with this,' he said, unclipping and lifting the telephone receiver with his abnormally gigantic hand, 'I can instantly call the Police National Computer switchboard. All I have to do then is read out a number plate of any car to the switchboard operator, and they'll tell me the owner of the car. Anyone want a demonstration?'

'Yes!' came the enthusiastic response from every kid watching.

'Really?'

'Yes!' came an even louder roar, several little pairs of fists punching the grass with excitement.

His eye turned to me again. 'Which is your car, madam?' he asked me, clearly revelling in the rapt attention.

Reluctantly, I pointed over to the cars in the field. 'That one.'

'The Jaguar?'

'No, the one next to that.'

He squinted to see it more clearly, shielding the glare of the sun with one massive hand. His face tightened as he tried to conceal the grin that threatened to erupt all over his face. 'You mean the Ford Escort?'

'Yes,' I confirmed.

'The pale blue one?'

'Yes.'

'With the orange front wings?'

'Yes.'

'And the red drivers' door?'

'Will you just get on with it?'

There was a ripple of laughter from the kids who sat around on the grass with crossed legs. I was uncomfortably aware that the juvenile crowd had swelled somewhat, and the policeman had quite an audience as he called the switchboard.

'Hello, Officer 5747, Tonbridge and Swanhurst, can I have a PNC check, please? Yes, the number is…' His forehead creased as he tried to make out the number. 'RKM715G.' There was a pause as the operator looked up the number.

I tried to keep it subtle, but did gesture with a tiny flick of my head that I wanted a word with him and he nodded. Luckily, he seemed quite quick on the uptake. Either that, or he thought he was on a promise.

'Sometimes takes a minute,' he told the kids, who seemed to barely be breathing as they waited. 'Ah, hello?' he said as the operator came back. As she spoke, his eyes went wide. 'Roger. Let me just confirm, that's Mrs Catriona *Athdara* Cameron of Frisky Pigeons, Ashfield Lane, Downscliffe, is that correct? Uh-huh, date-of-birth… Wow, 1944. As old as that, eh? Okay, thanks for your help.'

Constable Cropper – who was possibly about to become the *late* Constable Cropper if he wasn't careful – dropped the receiver back into its cradle and clipped it in place.

'Now, if you will all excuse me, I think Mrs Cameron would like to discuss some official police business with me.'

There was a uniform sigh of disappointment from the crowd.

'And no touching the motorcycle while I'm gone, you hear?' he said, waggling an accusing finger at a few likely suspects. 'Anyone who does, gets to spend the next ten years in prison.'

He extricated himself from the throng of kids, who had all started talking animatedly to each other as the constable absented himself. We strolled toward the perimeter of the playing field, which seemed to be the quietest place. Well, relatively speaking. The incessant big band music kept relentlessly playing, while children screamed and laughed and adults drank to Her Majesty's good health and complained vociferously about the weather. A group of fifteen or so young women, all dressed in jeans of various shades of blue and matching white t-shirts, were doing something akin to a can-can around the field. As they passed, I noted that all the shirts were printed with the same design: Downscliffe Ladies' Cricket Team. From their exuberance, I assumed that they had won yesterday's game against their bitter rivals, Priory Green, and were having an alcohol-fuelled raucous celebration today. There were certainly going to be some sore heads come the morning.

'Ten years in prison?' I queried the constable with a raised eyebrow, flicking hair away from my face so he could get the full effect of it, the gusty wind immediately blowing it back again. 'Tut-tut. That doesn't sound terribly professional.'

'Well, I'm not a very professional policeman. But you're absolutely right. I should've said borstal.'

'Did you hear about Jack Wimble?'

'I heard something. I gather he was taken ill just before I arrived. Hope it was nothing serious.'

'It certainly looked serious. Very, in fact. They thought it was a heart attack, but I caught a glimpse of him. His pupils were fully dilated and he was frothing at the mouth.'

'Isn't that…?'

'Poison, aye. I couldn't be sure without seeing a blood test, but I think it was Atropa belladonna – deadly nightshade.'

Constable Cropper chewed the inside of his cheek as he thought about this.

'I also saw Wally Moore immediately after it happened. He was watching the ambulancemen as they carried him away. He was smiling.'

'Smiling?'

'Aye. Now, that doesn't mean he was responsible, and on the evidence, it may be unlikely. I was with Wally for a good fifteen minutes beforehand and he never left the table. We were having a drink at one of the benches outside the beer tent. I was asking him about Veronica Castle.'

'Which tent was this?'

I pointed across the field. 'The Old Badger beer tent. Derek Tucker is there, if you'd like to speak with him.'

He took my arm, his hands powerful yet his touch gentle, as if he were handling the most fragile porcelain. 'Come with me. I don't think we can do a lot today. A lot of the regular police staff have the day off. Bank holiday for the jubilee, don't you know. And the rest are stretched thin, so unless there's an emergency of some kind, we won't get any action for a while.' He glanced at his watch. 'And it won't be too long before I have to head over to Priory Green and show my face at their jubilee day event.'

'No rest for the wicked,' I quipped.

'I hope you didn't mind me teasing you back there about your car and your middle name.'

'Oh, go away with you! It was just a bit of fun. If we cannae have a laugh, what can we do?'

'Join the Jubilee Celebration Committee?' he replied without missing a beat. 'So, Athdara? I have to confess, I've never come across that one before.'

'It means, "from the oak tree ford". I drive a Ford and once hit an oak tree so it's kind of appropriate.'

Apparently he couldn't argue with that logic. 'So, can I call you Athdara from now on?' he asked, and braced himself.

'You can call me Mrs Cameron, Constable Cropper,' I replied in an admonishing tone, but he could see I wasn't serious. 'But if no one else is around, I'm happy if you call me Catriona.'

'Catriona it is, then. Ah, here we are.'

The Old Badger beer tent seemed as busy as it had been before, but there was an extra buzz about the place now. Whether this was from the accumulation of alcohol loosening tongues and loosening inhibitions, or gossip over Jack Wimble's collapse, it was impossible to tell. I suspected it was a combination of the two. Quite a few had now spilled out and were sat around the park benches and on the grass. Plastic glasses were scattered around tables, some full, most empty, and many more lay discarded on the grass to be blown around in the breeze. A couple of entrepreneurial little boys were collecting them up in the hope of earning a few pence for them. I didn't rate their chances with the notoriously stingy Derek Tucker.

Derek must have been hidden away inside the beer tent as there was no sign of him, but we did see one of the barmaids-cum-waitresses standing just outside the door. It was the ginger-haired girl I had seen earlier. She was taking a long draw on a cigarette, its tip momentarily illuminating, before it was engulfed in smoke. Her hair was straight and shoulder length. Any exposed skin I could see, from her face to her wrists and ankles, was covered in freckles. She was carrying a little more weight than her colleague, but her freckly face was prettier than I'd given her credit for originally.

'If you're looking for dodgy Derek, he's inside,' she said as she took a final drag on the cigarette and stamped it out on the grass.

'Are you sure you're old enough to smoke that, young lady?' Constable Cropper asked sternly.

She replied with the kind of gesture normally reserved for rival fans at a football match. It was quite bold, I thought. Colin was certainly easygoing, as policemen went, but I wondered how he would react. The next thing I knew, she had flung her arms around his neck and was either being very friendly, or trying to kill him.

It turned out to be the former. They extricated

themselves from the almost unseemly hug and she stepped back, grinning from ear to ear.

'Jenny, you really shouldn't do that while I'm working.'

'Don't be such a putz, Lurch. You worried the fabric of society will break down if people see you getting a hug?'

Colin turned to me a little embarrassed. 'This is my baby sister, Jenny. Jenny, this is my friend, Catriona.'

I looked at him and then looked at her. Specifically, I looked at the matching ginger hair and wondered why I'd been so unutterably dense. Of course they were brother and sister. I mean, it was not as if ginger-haired people were ten a penny in the area. I was surprised when she also grabbed me and hugged me, not quite as ferociously as she had her brother, but with more affection than I was used to.

'Don't let him give you a hard time, Catriona. If he does, remind him that I used to beat him up when I was still a kid. And he knows I still could if I have a mind to.'

'She's not wrong, the six-foot-three policeman confirmed. 'Did you see what happened earlier?'

'You mean Jack Wimble? Yeah, everyone did. Certainly gave me the willies, I can tell you. Marianne was really upset. I thought she was going to faint. She's gone home now, so dodgy Derek is having to actually do some work. It *was* pretty shocking, though.'

'Catriona thinks he might've been poisoned,' the constable said, plucking his notebook from his pocket.

'No! That is so freaky-deaky, man. What makes you think that?'

'Some of the symptoms he had,' I explained. 'It looked like deadly nightshade, or something along those lines.'

'Did you see anyone around him who could have spiked his drink?' her brother asked, but her reaction was not encouraging.

'Yeah, about a hundred people, including me and including Derek.'

'Did you see Wally Moore nearby at all?'

She thought back, frowning with concentration. 'I don't think so. I don't know. Maybe. I wasn't standing there watching everybody. I was serving drinks.'

'That's fine,' he said in his lighter, "don't pressure the witness" voice. 'If you do think of anything, then let me know straightaway. I've got to head off to Priory Green now, but if you call the station they can pass on a message. Ask for Lucy. WPC Lucy Walraven.'

'Mum!' came a shout from behind me, and I turned to see a little time lord barrelling toward me, coat and scarf billowing in the air behind him. 'The competition is going to start.'

I looked at my watch and yes, it was nearly two. He looked up at me, eyes wide and pleading.

'Colin, I have to be heading off. Prior engagement,' I said with a gesture toward Fergus.

'Me too. I'll also enquire as to Jack Wimble's condition on the way.'

A Three Villages Mystery

'I gotta skitty,' Jenny said, tucking a packet of ten Silk Cut and a yellow box of Ship matches into her apron and heading back into the fray.

With a casual offhand salute, Constable Cropper headed in the opposite direction, back toward his waiting motorcycle and the gaggle of newfound fans.

I turned back to Fergus, his eyes expectant, an excited grin on his face. His long burgundy coat and stripey scarf were clarted in bits of dried grass, and I set about picking the worst of it off. 'Right, my young foostie loon, what do you say we go and try our luck at this fancy dress, eh?'

He grabbed my hand and practically dragged me to the fancy dress contest.

Twenty-One

There were a bakers' dozen of contestants in the fancy dress competition, none above the age of fourteen, the youngest appearing to be about five. All the costumes appeared to be handmade, and were striking in their diversity. Debbie's boys, Freddie and Arthur, otherwise known today as Stan Laurel and Oliver Hardy, were there and being fussed over by their mother. There was also what looked like a giant papier mâché sunflower waddling unsteadily about, a pitifully unconvincing Huckleberry Hound, a couple of Disney princesses, a cowboy, a Thunderbirds puppet (without strings), the Tin Man from Wizard of Oz, one of the mechanical men from the Robert's Robots TV show, covered in silver make-up with matching curly wig, a seven-year-old with a cigar and grubby raincoat who was either Columbo, or in dire need of a bath. There was also a miniature version of Queen Elizabeth II, with a cardboard crown which looked like a dog had chewed it and holding a sceptre that looked distinctly like a fireplace poker covered in Bacofoil, and a two-legged television set that was running around clattering into anyone and everyone in the vicinity.

They were certainly an eclectic bunch. Personally, my money was on the little Doctor Who, in his musty wig and floppy hat. But then again, I was perhaps just a smidge biased.

At that moment I heard the roar of a motorcycle firing up, and looked across to the small area behind the village hall. The sunlight glinted on the shiny white body of PC Cropper's police bike as he trundled it slowly through the crowds. It was amazing to me that at such a low speed, he didn't need to put a steadying foot down once. He waited at the car park entrance as a van passed, heading down toward the church, before he headed out onto the road. A moment later I lost sight of him, but the sound of the engine lingered for several seconds more, before being lost in the cacophony of brass band music and the screams of happy and excited children.

'Wotcha chick,' Debbie yelled over to me as she finished adjusting the cushion under Oliver Hardy's white button-down shirt.

'Hey sunshine,' I replied, guiding mini Tom Baker over to her so I could be equally annoying to my own son, picking off more grass, adjusting the scarf, checking the buttons on his wee waistcoat etc. He was sweltering under all those layers, his face flushed and glistening with little beads of sweat that he would periodically wipe away with his sleeve.

'Any more news?' Debbie asked.

'Not really, aside from public humiliation and ridicule towards me.'

'Average Monday then, eh? Who was it? Want me to break someone's legs for you?'

'No, I can't say that I was really complaining about it.'

It took all of two seconds for this to sink in. 'Oh, cosying up to your policeman "friend", are we?'

'Hardly, there were about twenty kids present. No, he ran a licence plate check on my car, so now knows just about everything about me, including my age and my middle name.'

'I didn't know you had a middle name.'

'I don't tend to use it very often.'

'What is it?'

'It's not important.'

'Catriona,' Debbie said slowly, stretching every syllable of the name almost to breaking point. 'We have no secrets, do we?'

I sighed. 'Athdara.'

She burst out laughing. 'What kind of a name is that?'

'It's what I was given when I was born! I mean, it's not like I had much choice in the matter.'

'I've got just two words for you girl: deed poll. That's all I'm saying on the subject.' Debbie turned away, as if facing the other direction meant that I wouldn't know she was trying not to wet herself laughing.

A Three Villages Mystery

'Ladies and gentlemen, boys and girls,' a distinguished voice said, amplified by a loudhailer I had the distinct impression had been left over from the Second World War. Or possibly the First. 'Would all the contestants line up on the stage, please?'

The "stage" appeared to be a line of rickety wooden fruit & veg crates in front of the three judges. They looked barely strong enough to take the weight of the children, and I imagined how much more entertaining it would be if some of the adults could take part. They'd be smashed to matchwood.

'That's you, loon,' I said quietly to Fergus. 'Break a leg.' He looked round at me in confusion. 'It means good luck.'

He ran over to the stage and joined Laurel and Hardy. Debbie sidled over next to me. 'Is it stupid that I'm really nervous for them?' she asked.

'Not at all. I feel the same way. Fergs has been really looking forward to this.'

'I'm afraid of what Ronnie and Reggie will do if they don't win. Probably tie the judge's eyebrows together.'

Now it was my turn to stifle a laugh. The Kray twins was a new moniker for her boys. I wondered whether these were pre-planned, or completely off the cuff. If it was the latter, it was a rare gift indeed.

The distinguished man, sporting a bushy moustache, eyebrows that Dennis Healey would've been proud of and a truly tragic combover, was one of the panel of three judges. He went along the line, stooped over, handing out numbers for each child to pin to his or her costume. He was slightly puzzled when he came to Laurel and Hardy, and had to quickly consult with his colleagues as to whether group entries were permissible. Fortunately, they were, and a major incident was narrowly averted. I dreaded to think what Debbie might have done if there was a problem. Probably insert his megaphone somewhere decidedly uncomfortable.

The judges huddled together, speaking in hushed tones and occasionally pointing at one of the anxious children who stood there, quivering with nerves and excitement. But mostly nerves. I was no better, the butterflies swirling around in my stomach more like buffalos.

'Oh Catriona, there you are, my love,' a woman's voice said from behind.

I turned to see a vision of blue gingham, topped with fiercely-curled hair. 'Hello Maureen. It's been a lovely day, hasn't it?'

'It has. Stressful, I can tell you, but a jolly good day, indeed. I was wondering…'

I held up a hand. 'Don't worry, I'm just staying until the end of the fancy dress, then I'll be over to the baking contest tent. Fergus is in this competition.'

'Oh is he?' she asked excitedly, and peered at the bizarre line of contestants.

They were all facing away from us, looking at the three judges who continued to make notes, glancing up and down every so often. They seemed to be taking an awfully long time, and I had a crazy urge to run up there, grab my baby and run away. He hated being on display like this. As much as he had wanted to take part and emulate his hero, he would be on the verge of panic the whole time.

'Which one is your lad, then?'

'The Doctor Who, in the big burgundy coat and the stripey scarf.'

'Oh so it is! Doesn't he look adorable?'

She wasn't going to get any argument from me.

There was a sudden change amongst the judges, and they had a final consultation before the distinguished man with exuberant facial hair stood again. He blew into the loudhailer three times, a long, keening wail of feedback coming from the device that caused everyone in a fifty-yard radius to wince.

'Oops. Apologies for that, ladies and gentlemen, boys and girls. I think we have decided on our top three. Haven't we?' he asked, checking one more time with his fellow judges. They nodded solemnly and he continued. 'Yes, apparently we are all in agreement and ready to reveal the results.' Sadly, he had none of the inadvertently comedic charm of the master of ceremonies who had opened the event.

'Oh, I do wish that confounded man would hurry up,' Maureen fretted, looking at her watch again.

'We've still got a few minutes left,' I said, trying to calm her down. I was nervous enough for the both of us anyway, without her starting her shenanigans. More than that, something was bothering me. I had put it down to nerves over the fancy dress and anxiety over judging the baking contest, but there was something nagging away in a quiet, dusty corner of my brain; something that I couldn't quite put my finger on. Every time I felt it come tantalisingly within my reach, it would sink back into the recesses of my mind. It surfaced again for a moment.

'I am happy to announce that in third place…'

And it was gone again, and this time I knew it had, for now at least, sunk deeper into my subconscious beyond my reach.

'The very inventive television set costume, worn by Luke Johnson. Congratulations young man, and please approach to collect your prize.'

I sighed, half with relief that Fergus's dream wasn't yet over, and partly because I'd have settled for third place. Third is better than no place at all. The television set wobbled unsteadily up to the judges, unceremoniously knocking a fairy princess clear off the stage as it went, and the distinguished man handed over a small bag of sweets.

'And in second place, Columbo, as worn by Mark Wickens. Congratulations young fellow-me-lad. Would you step forward?'

'You have got to be kidding me,' Debbie hissed through clenched teeth. 'He gets second place for wearing an old flashers' mac?'

'Don't forget the cigar,' I whispered back. 'I'm sure that's what swung it.'

The shambling detective ambled forwards, and

collected a slightly larger bag of sweets.

'And finally, it gives me great pleasure...'

'Oh, just get on with it, you tiresome little man,' Maureen moaned, and the man faltered for just an instant, the words coming out slightly louder than she had intended.

'Yes, great pleasure to... Where was I?' he queried his fellow judges, one of whom held up a scrap of paper for him to read.

I thought Maureen was going to explode.

'The winner of the Jubilee Celebration Fancy Dress Contest is... is... is...'

'Oh, for the love of—'

'Her Majesty Queen Elizabeth II herself, expertly portrayed by Clare Pemble.'

I saw Fergus's shoulders slump, and my heart broke, just a little.

'That settles it. It's all political,' Debbie fumed.

'Oh well. Maybe next time,' Maureen said brightly. Now, shall we?'

She was in severe danger of being throttled where she stood. 'Just give me a minute with my bairn,' I snapped back, hearing the note of irritation in my own voice, and quite frankly not really caring. Sometimes, a message had to be sent which was not open to interpretation.

Fergus came stomping toward me, a small half smile on his face. He shrugged phlegmatically when he got to me. 'We'll do better next time, Mum. When's the next one?'

A Jubilee Murder

'The next jubilee? That'll be in twenty-five years' time I reckon, which by my calculation should be 2002.'

'Good. Plenty of time to get it right. I'm just not dressing up as the Queen,' he said and did his best to wink at me. He'd never been very good at winking, half his face screwing up but the eye resolutely remaining open.

Maureen was now standing at a respectable distance, not wishing to encroach on the private moment between mother and child, lest she incur any more of my Caledonian wrath, but she might as well have been jumping up and down and waving a "hurry up Catriona" banner.

'I need to go judge this cake contest, sweetheart,' I said, brushing a lock of mouldy hair away from his face. I hoped I hadn't given him nits with that wig. 'Will you be okay staying close to Auntie Debbie for a bit?'

'Sure. Bring some of your cake home, Mum, it's bound to be loads better than theirs.'

'Then we'll have two,' I said. One each!'

I gave him a kiss and a cuddle and left him with Debbie while I tramped off to judge this contest.

Two, I thought. We'll have *two* cakes to get through. The number was important somehow. It related to that nagging little idea that was still swimming around on the edge of my subconscious. Two. Veronica. She was attacked from behind. Someone had swept a cord around her neck and tightened it in the blink of an eye. But all that would do was crush her windpipe. It wouldn't kill her instantly. She would have defended herself, but she couldn't for some reason. Why not? Something was stopping her, but her hands can't have been tied. Maybe she had been drugged, but that would leave some evidence in the toxicology report. Why go to all the trouble of making it look like suicide if the truth would come out in a few days anyway?

She must have been held in place by someone else, someone enveloping her in their arms so she couldn't move. Couldn't fight back.

It was with a sickening feeling that I realised how it had happened. There was no other explanation that would fit the facts. There were two of them.

I was almost there. There was just one more piece of the puzzle to uncover.

Twenty-Two

It was only when we got to the marquee that I realised Maureen might have had a point, and that time was indeed short. The temperature outside was just edging into the upper twenties, but under the canvas it was closer to thirty, and still rising. Lines of folding chairs had been set up in front of two trellis tables and, somewhat incongruously, an ornate art deco lectern from which I was to speak.

'It's all set up for you, my dear,' Maureen cooed. 'We're all ready for you to start the judging, and then say a few well-chosen words when you've decided on the top three. Is that all right, duck?'

I smiled and nodded nervously as I looked around, still unable to fathom why people around these parts insisted on calling me a duck.

The chairs were beginning to fill with eager contestants and their families, the grass beneath their feet being slowly trampled into submission. On the tables were a line of cakes, all broadly similar and in varying

227

degrees of neatness. Some were, I had to admit, finished to a high level. However, there were others that looked like cow pats that had been dropped from several feet up to splat onto a cake board.

'They're all very good, don't you think, Catriona? The ladies of the village have really done 'emselves proud with this selection.'

'They have indeed,' I echoed, determining that diplomacy was probably the wisest option here, if I wanted to get out alive.

At the centre of the display was my own offering, raised higher than the rest and setting an example of how this recipe should be presented. At least I assumed that was the theory. I really hoped no one actually tasted it. What if it turned out to be substantially below par? I had rather assumed that the quality here would be fairly low, but this was evidently not the case for the most part. Discounting the cow pats, a few looked exceptionally good. At least, they would have done if it were not for the heat. My idea of piling up curled chocolate shavings had seemed a good idea at the time, but they were beginning to sag a little. It wouldn't be long before the cake resembled one of the aforementioned dung heaps.

Someone had quite sensibly purloined a couple of desk fans, probably from the village hall, and had them blowing air over the selection. A cable snaked across the ground, almost buried in the grass and disappearing under the tent wall. I had no idea where the fans were being powered from, but just hoped that the whole marquee wasn't about to go up in flames, or even more entertainingly, electrocute everyone inside.

'Catriona, my dear,' came an unwelcome voice.

'Mrs Popplewell,' I replied brightly, plastering a smile on my face that made it look as if I was gurning like a ventriloquist's dummy. 'The ladies do seem to have excelled themselves, don't they?'

'Oh yes, dear. We do pride ourselves on the calibre of baking talent within the village of Downscliffe, and upholding the old traditions.'

'Clearly. Have you yourself submitted an entry?'

She stepped back suddenly, her nose going up in indignation and nostrils flaring. 'As a member of the Jubilee Celebration Committee, I hardly think that would be appropriate. My baking skills are somewhat advanced, so naturally I would stand an exceptionally high chance of winning, and that would not look ethical at all.'

'Oh no, not at all,' I agreed, nodding as if my head were about to fall off. That was me telt.

'I was just saying to Mrs Johnson,' Maureen interrupted, knowing what Mrs Popplewell was like and trying to avoid an incident where a chocolate cake might get slammed in her face. 'We're very lucky that you graciously agreed to step in and 'elp us out.'

'Oh yeah, life saver, aren't you, Caty?' That was Barbara Johnson, whom I had rarely spoken to away from the school gates.

'Not at all. Glad I could help.' I wasn't glad. Not in the least. I was hating every tortuous minute of this. 'Is there any word on Mr Wimble? Shocking business.'

'Oh shocking, shocking,' Barbara agreed.

'Lucky escape for him if he did have a heart attack,' Maureen blurted, and then clapped her hands to her mouth. 'Oh I'm sorry. That's a dreadful thing to say.'

I waved a hand dismissively. 'Why a lucky escape?'

'Well you know I don't like to be a gossip,' she said quietly, leaning in closer, 'but the way I 'ear it, Kitty found out he was carrying on with poor old Veronica.'

'What? You mean they'd picked up where they left off thirty years ago?'

'Oh yeah, that's what I was 'earing, and Kitty wasn't best pleased about it. Not best pleased at all.'

'Really, Mrs Bishop,' Mrs Popplewell chided, 'there's no need for malicious gossip when one of the protagonists has so recently passed away so tragically, and the other is fighting for his very life as we speak.'

'But it's strange, don't you think?' Maureen persisted. 'The two people who had that affair all those year ago, are now dead or dying.'

It *was* strange, and I now had more than an inkling of what the explanation was. But there was still that last annoying piece of the puzzle to reveal, the last little jigsaw piece to fit into place.

'Perhaps we should begin the judging?' I asked, hoping to avert a full-on fistfight between Maureen and Mrs Popplewell. Then again, it might be worth it. I knew who I'd be rooting for.

'Good idea, let's just get on with it,' Barbara

intervened. 'You two can slug it out after.'

Mrs Popplewell put on her best snooty face, which was just one of an entire extended repertoire, while Maureen and I moved over to the line of cakes and moved slowly down until we reached the first. Fourteen cakes, I thought. I would need to have at least one bite of each. If I ended today without being sick as a dog, it would be something of a miracle.

Maureen fished a piece of paper from her handbag. 'Ah, the first one 'ere is by Mrs Beecher of Primrose Cottage.'

The cake didn't look too bad, I thought. The chocolate hadn't been tempered, the surface dull and flat, and not especially appetising. I pushed a sharp knife into it, and pushed, and pushed. Eventually I managed to hack my way through and take a thin, crumbly slice. It seemed that Mrs Beecher had worked on the assumption that more chocolate was better, and had not bothered with any other ingredients, save for a few randomly scattered lumps of biscuit. I dutifully made appreciative cooing noises as I chewed on it, and the rotund woman in the front row suddenly looked quite pleased with herself.

Onto the next one, a sagging cow pat of a cake by Mrs Dute of Treetops, followed by an offering by Mrs Jeffery of Meadow View. By the time we got to Mrs Gasp of Woodside, I was thoroughly sick of chocolate cake, but continued gamely. They should've asked Debbie to do this. She could shovel cake away like a stoker shovelling coal on a steam train.

A Three Villages Mystery

I glanced at the piece of paper Maureen was holding. By now, it was stained with chocolate, but the words were still perfectly legible.

'What's that?' I enquired, looking at the list, something stirring at the back of my mind.

'This, my lovely?' She looked down at the piece of paper. 'Why, it's my list of contest entrants, deary. It's 'ow I know whose cake is whose.'

I stared at the list of names. B. Prim, D. Tree, J. Mead, G. Wood. 'But that doesn't give the list of names.'

'No, but it's just my sort of shorthand. It's how I learned it in school. The contestants' initial, followed by the name of their 'ouse. Or a shortened version of it, anyways. I know it's not how everyone does it, but it works fine for me. Always has done. Are you all right, duck?'

I quickly reached into my own shoulder bag and retrieved my purse, inside which was another scrap of paper. A till receipt. I looked at it for the thousandth time.

'You said you learned that method in school, right?' I asked.

'Yes, I dare say I'm not the only one.'

'The same school that Veronica Castle went to?'

'Yes. She were in the same class as me, in fact.'

'But her name wasn't Veronica then, was it? It was Bessie Moore.'

She nodded, and I became aware of a disquieted hubbub from the expectant crowd.

'I thought this was a name,' I said, shaking the fist

that held the scrap of paper. 'T. Wills. I thought it meant Terry Willes, from the top of Ashfield Lane, but it didn't. It meant…'

My brain made a belated attempt to catch up with my mouth, and the truth revealed itself to me. It was the awful, terrible truth that perhaps my subconscious had been suppressing, but now there was no escaping it.

The realisations came quickly, one after the other as the pieces of the puzzle slipped easily and logically into place.

Another image flashed into my head: the gleaming white moulded bodywork of Constable Cropper's motorcycle as it gingerly edged its way through the crowds until it sat waiting at the car park entrance. A van had driven past. A white transit van, heading down toward the church. At the time I saw it, something had not seemed quite right. Something about that tableau jarred my subconscious and it was only now that I realised what it was.

Why would a transit van be going down to the church today of all days? It was a public holiday. It was jubilee day. The whole country was out celebrating, and yet this one van was heading down to an empty country church.

He was the one. He had murdered Veronica, or Bessie, or whatever name she had chosen to go by. He was going down to that church, and there was only one reason I could think of for that: to destroy evidence. He had already broken in once, and was now going back to finish the job.

I knew what I had to do.

There was one cake left, so I hacked into it like a starving hunter hacking into a fresh carcass, and took a quick bite. 'Mmm, yummy,' I mumbled through a mouthful of stodgy cake, brown flakes tickling my chin as they fluttered to the ground.

'Oh good,' Maureen said with relief. She clearly didn't have a clue of what was going on. 'D'you think you've got a top three for us, Catriona, dear?'

'Yes, that one, that one and that one,' I said as I brushed sticky crumbs from my fingers.

'Oh! Um… In what order?'

'Third, second, first,' I said, pointing to the three cakes in order. 'Thank you for coming everyone. Now, I must dash.'

With my head down, studiously avoiding making eye contact with any of the befuddled and appalled onlookers, I strode from the marquee and back out into the sunshine. It was still a blisteringly hot day, but it almost felt cool as I stepped out into the fresh air, away from the oppressive heat within the tent. As soon as I felt the warmth on my cheeks, I whipped my sunglasses back into place.

I needed to find Debbie, and held a hand up to my eyes to shield them from the blazing mid-afternoon sun. There seemed to be even more people crammed into the playing field now, playing the fairground games, weaving their way between the lines of classic cars, queuing for ice creams and candy floss, staggering around the two beer tents.

But there was no sign of Debbie. I needed her, now more than ever. I did see Dotty and Gemma from The Old Badger and hurried over to them, nearly breaking my ankle in the process as I lurched first one way, then the other. It was not Catriona at her most elegant, but I didn't have time for finesse.

'Hey Dotty, hold up chuck.'

She looked round and for some reason, didn't look pleased to see me, but the answer soon became clear enough.

'If he's sent you to order me back to that kitchen, you can go tell him he can just—'

'No, no, Dotty,' I pleaded, holding up my hands. 'I haven't seen Derek for a while. I'm looking for my friend, Debbie Dugdale. Have you seen her? It is rather important.'

She looked a little deflated, as if she had been working herself up to have a fight and been denied. 'Oh. Well, in that case, never mind. Your friend Debbie, you say? Well, I can't be sure, mind, but I think I saw her and her boys down at the far end of the field. Queuing for that go-kart ride, they were.'

'Go-karts. Right. Got it.' I headed off, thanking Dotty and telling her to make sure they had a great time away from the kitchen.

Sure enough, after battling my way through the hordes of celebrating people, I found Debbie at the go-karts. She was stood there with Arthur, her youngest by a full eighteen minutes, watching two small and noisy karts go flying around a taped off circuit. They sounded like angry wasps, making a squealing wail every time they went past.

Fergus caught sight of me and, as cool as James Hunt, gave me a salute as he screamed by. It seemed that in the space of an hour, he had lost his fondness for two wheels, and was now a solid devotee of four-wheeled open cockpit racing. I was pleased to see that he was more than holding his own against Freddie, also known as terrible twin No 1, and was actually starting to pull away from him.

'Hey there, foxy mama,' Debbie shouted above the whine of two-stroke engines. 'Did it all go okay?'

'Don't know. Didn't wait to find out. Listen, I know how it was done.'

'Who? Did what?'

'Veronica. I finally figured it out. Now, I need your help.'

'Far out. Who was it?'

'Never mind that for now. I need you to get to a phone and contact Constable Cropper. You'll have to call the station. Ask for WPC…' I stared up at the clear blue sky for a moment as I tried to remember her name, then it came to me. 'WPC Lucy Walraven. She can get in touch with Colin.'

'Okay, and then what?' She waved her hand at Fergus and Freddie, beckoning them to pull up and come back to her.

'Tell him to meet me at the church. The killer is there, trying to destroy the evidence.'

'Well I'm coming with you then.'

'No, I need you to make that call, and then keep the boys safe. I don't want you coming to the church.'

'But—'

'No, absolutely not. Please, just look after Fergus for me. And do not, under any circumstances, come to the church. Just get Colin there as fast as you can.'

'All right,' Debbie said uneasily. 'But you take care.'

'Don't worry about me. I'll be fine as soon as Colin gets there.'

I gave her a quick hug, turned, and strutted up the field, sticking to the extreme perimeter to avoid the crowds.

I had to get to St Luke's Church.

Twenty-Three

When I parked Ernie up outside the church, my suspicions were confirmed. The white transit van I had seen go past earlier was there, parked on the threadbare grass under the yew trees, their lower branches brushing its roof. The area was deserted, the van apparently empty. In the distance, I could hear the muffled, echoing sound of the public address system at the jubilee celebration, and the sound of singing. The brass band music had now given way to pop music. Presumably whoever had been in charge of the sound system had been lynched and replaced by someone with an ear for more modern sounds. At this moment, the revellers were being treated to Showaddywaddy's hit, Under the Moon of Love, so admittedly not *that* modern.

I glanced around, but could see no one. The birds chirped in the trees, branches were tossed back and forth in the wind. Dead leaves, left over from the previous autumn, danced in extravagant eddies on the ground. The rich green leaves of virgin wheat swayed rhythmically in the fields. It was so quiet here, so peaceful, the breeze offering a dramatic soundtrack. In this idyllic setting, it was hard to believe that any crime could ever have been committed, let alone one so brutal as coldblooded murder.

I looked over to the cottage, but there was no sign of Celia Fernsby-Brown. Her car was also missing. She was probably off, "borrowing" some milk or sugar or tea or gin or whatnot from someone up Ashfield Lane, or helping to push her husband's bubble car back from the playing field.

The transit van had been here for a while and the stub bonnet was cool to the touch. I took one last glance around before trying the drivers' side door. The mechanism clunked and released, the door sliding open, just a fraction. I slid it open fully and peered inside. It was dirty, like it had not been cleaned since it was new. There was a musty scent to the interior, and a sweetness as well. The smell of old pipe tobacco lingered in the cloth seats and orange curtains tied back against the rear partition. A week-old newspaper was stuffed under the drivers' seat and an old, crunched up can of Top Deck Shandy lay in the well between the torn seats. There was also a rolled-up puffer jacket stuffed in there, which had been black at some point in the past, but had greyed from too long sitting in the sunlight, and too much exposure to plaster dust.

I wasn't sure what I'd been expecting to find. Maybe a length of cord with a note tied to it saying "murder weapon" would've been handy. No, life wasn't quite that easy.

The jacket caught my attention again. It looked innocuous enough, but was ever so slightly thicker than it should be. After another surreptitious glance around to make sure I wasn't being watched, I reached in and tugged at the jacket, prizing it from the space between the seats. It unravelled as I pulled, something emerging and dropping to the van's floor with a thud. I let go of the jacket immediately and stared. Lying in the dusty footwell, littered with Opal Fruit wrappers, was a cross; a golden cross around six inches long.

Well, there was no doubt anymore. This was the cross that had been stolen from the church after the break-in on Saturday night.

I didn't feel any sense of triumph, no elation or excitement. This merely confirmed a truth that until this moment I had hoped – prayed – I was wrong about. But there was no denying it now.

It was time for me to confront this demon.

I retrieved the cross and slipped it into my shoulder bag, making sure not to touch it with my bare fingers, and crossed the roadway to climb the three or four steps to the churchyard. The tower loomed above me, stretching high into the sky and dwarfing the nave. There was a scent as I entered the building, old paper mixed with older timber and wood polish, along with ancient candle wax and lilies.

I passed the noticeboard just inside the entrance and went into the main part of the church. It was almost empty. Almost. Towards the far end, a man was standing on one of the pews, pinning a nice new electrical cable to the wall that ran the length of the nave.

He looked round when he heard my echoing footsteps on the floor.

'Wotcha Ginger,' the moustachioed man said, a smoking pipe clamped between his teeth, his voice echoing through the empty chamber.

'Hello Tony,' I replied, without anger or fear. Only sorrow. Even with all the evidence that I had found, I had still, on some level, hoped and prayed that it would not be Debbie's husband I would be confronting. If I was going to be honest, I had been in no doubt since I deciphered the scrap of paper. T. Wills did not refer to Terry Willes, but Tony from The Willows.

'What brings you to this neck of the woods, eh darlin'?'

'I think you know. I know what you did, Tony. I finally figured it out today.'

'You *think* you know, but you don't really. You're just guessing, doll. And you'd be wrong.'

'Where is she?' I asked.

'Where's who?'

'Marianne.'

There was the swoosh of a curtain and I looked round. Emerging from the vestry was Marianne, strolling casually toward me.

'Give it up, babe,' she said. 'She knows. The only question I have is, how?'

She had changed out of her waitress's uniform of

neat black skirt and white blouse, and now wore lilac slacks with a tight mauve polo neck sweater. A long gold chain was draped around her neck, a crucifix pendant hanging almost mockingly over her chest.

'There you are, Marianne,' I greeted her. 'You were the daughter of Veronica Castle, or Bessie Moore when she gave you up. But I bet your name wasn't Marianne back then, was it?'

'I'm Marianne now. That child died a long time ago.'

'Of course. You were the mistake that was never meant to happen. The result of an illicit affair between one of the notables of the village, and an impressionable teenage girl who made the mistake of falling in love with him. Given up for adoption and tossed from one foster home to another. Never settling, never forming any real relationships or attachments, but always aware of the growing hate within you, and resentment towards your parents.'

'We all have to take responsibility for our actions,' Marianne responded. 'Even you. Sooner or later, you'll have to go back to Aberdeen and deal with those issues, instead of running away.'

'I'm sure I will. It has to come eventually.'

'Tell me something,' she asked, leaning her backside against a pew, the ancient timber creaking as she did so. 'What gave us away?'

I smiled. 'It was all about revenge, wasn't it? You wanted to make the people who wronged you pay. You saw the life that your mother had created for herself, becoming the big media star, becoming rich, becoming famous and loved by all, and you hated her for it. You followed her here to this village, took a part-time job in the local pub and lodged in a local house. You knew you couldn't do this alone, so you seduced this fool,' I said, gesturing to Tony, who had by now come down from the pew and was stood a few feet from me. I noted the length of cord in his hand.

'She didn't seduce me,' he responded. 'And it wasn't *all* about revenge. There was also the subject of Veronica's will. I'll give you three guesses, Ginger, who was the sole recipient?'

'I assumed as much. So, you'd stand to inherit your mother's fortune as well, wouldn't you Marianne? All very neat. And then you found out that Veronica had once again begun a secret relationship with Jack. They were blissfully carrying on with each other, and the sacrifice that you had been forced to make had been for nothing.'

'You have no idea what it was like, Catriona,' Marianne said, examining her fingernails at arms' length. 'It felt like I'd been stabbed, and the blade was slowly being twisted inside me. I couldn't let that continue. Not after all they'd done.'

'But she was onto you. She knew you and Tony were having this secret affair, although I doubt she realised what your intentions were. You lured her to this church, didn't you?' I continued. 'Last Friday, you lured her here. This was when you revealed yourself to her, making her believe that her long lost child was willing to be her faithful daughter again. And then – and this is the sickest part – you hugged your mother, wrapping your arms around her while lover boy here came up behind and strangled her with a length of electrical cable. In cold blood, you held her tight so she couldn't struggle and injure herself, because you had to make it look like a suicide back at her house. It couldn't look like murder, not with you as the sole recipient in her will.'

'It was actually easier than I thought. I'd never killed anyone before.'

'But you have since. Your little stunt today was what gave you away. There were fifty odd people around who could have poisoned Jack Wimble, so you thought suspicion would never fall on you. But it was how you chose to kill him that gave you away. I remembered that you are a botany student at Swanhurst East College. You would know precisely what to look for, and where to find Atropa belladonna. You also knew the quantity to use to prolong his suffering and cause the most unpleasant death.'

'Very clever, Catriona. You seem to have it all worked out.'

'But things started to go wrong almost from the start. Tony here, never exactly the sharpest tool in the box, used some of his own electrical cable to murder Veronica. As soon as you realised that someone was looking into her death, he had to come back here and retrieve the rest of it. That was the real reason why he broke in on Saturday night. He just took the gold cross and messed up the place to make it look like a burglary. And I'm guessing that after that, you told him he had to remove *all* traces of the cable in this church, anything that could connect the two of you to Veronica's death. Am I right?'

Neither of them said anything.

'So that's why you're both in here today, tying up the loose ends, as it were. I'm just surprised that the vicar wasn't here to stop you. Unless…'

Marianne smiled. She was such a pretty girl, who had inherited her mother's stunning looks, but right now that smile was one of the ugliest things I'd ever seen.

'You've killed him as well? But he—'

'Was complicit!' she snapped. 'He was the one who had me spirited away. He was as much to blame as they were. But no, if you're worried about poor old Reverend Cackett, he's not dead, but he's not quite himself, either.'

'What do you mean?'

She laughed, with a shake of her head. 'In the end, it was so easy. Did you happen to see the fresh lemonade stall at the jubilee celebration? I thought he might appreciate some refreshment. Lemonade, with an added dash of henbane, mandrake and jimsonweed. Mix them together and you get an effect similar to LSD, but a sufficient dose can destroy the mind. You see Catriona, it wasn't enough to make him live with his demons inside his head. They had to be real to him, and now they are. He will live with those demons for the rest of his life.'

I stared at her in astonishment and horror. I knew she was a murderer. I knew that she had wanted revenge.

A Three Villages Mystery

What I hadn't realised until this moment, was how utterly insane she was.

'And you're happy to go along with this, Tony?' I asked, noting that he now held the cord in both hands, repeatedly pulling it taut and relaxing it again.

He shrugged. 'This way I get to be rich, and have a beautiful girl on my arm. Who's gonna say no to that?'

'You have a beautiful wife and two beautiful boys.'

'Yeah, but I still wouldn't be rich.'

'Is that true, Tony?' a voice said from the doorway, and my heart sank. Debbie stood there, her face ashen, shoulders sagging.

'What are you doing here?' Tony demanded, eyes wide. 'You shouldn't have come. We… We're just playing a game, right Ginger?' he laughed nervously.

'You murdered Veronica? Oh my God, Tony. What have you done, you idiot?'

'No-no, tell her, Ginge. Tell her it's a game.'

I looked to Debbie, tears welling in my eyes. 'I'm sorry, I can't. I wish I could change things, but yes, Debs, he did. He did it for her.' I pointed at Marianne, who was looking bored by proceedings.

'Oh, let's just kill them both, babe,' she said, and strode down the nave toward Debbie.

I felt Tony's body behind me, pressing into my back, and caught a glimpse of the cord as it came down my face. I flung my hands up to grab it, just as the length of cable went tight. My fingertips were caught between the cord and my throat and I wrenched at it. Tony was stronger.

Much stronger, pulling tight on the two ends of the cord and I felt my windpipe being constricted. Somewhere in the distance was a scream, but my head was being yanked back and I couldn't see where it came from.

I had a few seconds to contemplate my own stupidity in coming here alone, and for inadvertently involving Debbie. In a crazy final few moments, I experienced a tiny crumb of satisfaction as I imagined that we would haunt this place together. I just wished I'd had a chance to say goodbye to Fergus, to hug him one last time.

The pressure on my throat was suddenly released and I dropped to the floor, sprawling on the cold, hard flagstones. Everything was a blur, but I heard the smack of flesh against flesh, and Tony's voice as he cried out in pain. I caught a glimpse of something: polished silver buttons on dark fabric.

I half lay on the floor, the cold stone giving me something on which to focus, the chill reminding me that I was still alive.

A few moments later I felt hands on my shoulders and had a dreadful thought that the cord would once again find its way around my neck and finish the job.

'Catriona? Catriona? Are you okay?' It was a man's voice, but not Tony's.

'Colin?' I croaked.

'The one and only. Hang on, be right back.'

With my vision beginning to clear, I could make out two figures at the far end of the aisle, one kneeling atop the other. Debbie had Marianne pinned face down, her knee painfully driving into the younger woman's back. She also had a fistful of her hair, which she held firmly, pulling so hard that Marianne's head was being yanked back at an unnatural angle.

Colin got to them and crouched down. 'It's okay, Mrs Dugdale, I've got her now.'

Debbie looked round at him and was clearly thinking about breaking the young woman's neck, but relented and released the knotted bunch of hair. Her head immediately cracked into the hard floor and she shrieked in pain.

'Oops,' Debbie muttered, and pulled her body away so the policeman could cuff her as well. She came over to me and sank down the pew next to me. 'Wotcha chick.'

'I'm sorry Debs,' I croaked, and swallowed several times to lubricate my throat. 'I never meant for you to find out this way.'

'Oh, don't be a bunny. Better I find out now than… Well, it would've helped if I'd found out before we were married, but at least I got Satan's minions out of it, so it's not all bad.'

'Are the boys all okay? Fergus? Is he—'

'Fergus is fine. I dropped all three boys off at your house first. Glad I did. I wouldn't want them to see their dad like that.' She stared across at Tony, lying on the floor, his hands cuffed behind his back, blood congealing in the moustache and coating the lower half of his face. It seemed that Colin had been a little less than gentle while restraining him, and I didn't have a problem with that.

A moment later, Constable Cropper returned and crouched beside us. 'I've just been in touch with the station. Back up should be here any minute. Are you both okay? Do you need an ambulance?'

'Bless you, no,' I said, touching his arm.

'He might need one,' Debbie said, glaring at Tony's prone form.

'I don't think I hit him too hard,' Colin said, looking nervously at the blood on the man's face.

'No, I mean for when I'm finished with him.'

'Who is this character?'

'Who is he? He's my stupid, useless, cheating, couldn't-find-his-own-backside-without-a-map-and-a-compass husband! Soon to be ex-husband. And I'm taking the house and the kids and the car,' she shouted, her face as red as mine gets when I've just climbed a hill on a hot day. 'In twenty years, when you get out of jail, you can live in your stupid, stinking van!'

Colin leaned back and blew the air between his teeth. 'Okay, I'm glad we've got her on our side. And the other woman? Who's she?'

'Veronica Castle's daughter,' I explained, my voice feeling and sounding stronger now. 'She hated her parents, and stood to inherit Veronica's estate.'

He shook his head. 'Unbelievable. You know, CID are going to have some questions. You think you're up to answering them down at the nick? I'll be there as well. You'll be just fine.'

'Of course. Colin, I think Reverend Cackett is here as well. He's probably in the vestry. She told me she'd drugged him. Please, see if he's okay.'

There was a distant peal of two-tone sirens, that quickly grew louder as they approached.

'Don't worry, I'll go check now,' Colin said, heaving himself to his feet.

He smiled, nodded to us both and jogged down the aisle and through to the vestry where he disappeared.

'Looks like that's our evening sorted,' Debbie sighed. 'All because of that traitorous can't-keep-it-in-his-trousers moron over there!'

Despite everything, I couldn't help but smile. 'Will it be okay to drop all three boys over to your mum's in Reydon?'

'Sure. She'll be convinced I've been arrested, and I'd hate to think what she's going to do with *him*,' she said, pointing her finger angrily at Tony, 'when she finds out. We could have another murder in the village.'

There was a crunch of gravel outside as three panda cars skidded to a halt on the loose ground.

The last few days were going to take some explaining.

Twenty-Four

Spending the evening in a police interrogation room was not how I had envisioned my day panning out when I woke up that morning. Looking around, I had to admit that this was a thoroughly miserable place. The walls were bare breeze blocks, painted a dull and thoroughly depressing cream, decades of grime filling every little cranny. Pipes ran along them, umpteen layers of paint filling in details, rusty stains running down them to form dried puddles on the drab, olive green floor. There was a smell to the room, a mixture of bleach and something altogether more unpleasant. Above was a single light. It wasn't a bare lightbulb, but for all the good the conical shade did it might as well have been. There was a single table in the centre of the room, with four chairs, two on each side.

Debbie and I sat on one side, while Colin and his inspector sat on the other. We had been there for almost an hour, explaining everything we had found out. Things had gotten a little awkward when it had come to our unauthorised entry to Veronica's house, but considering the outcome, it looked like the inspector was willing to gloss over that part since our intentions were clearly benign. He was a tall, skinny man, who looked like he would snap if you bent him in two, but I suspected he was actually tougher than that. He was in the advanced stages of balding, with a smooth, shiny head, but a mass of bushy dark hair around the sides and the back.

We talked until early evening, explaining how the missing Triumph Spitfire was our first clue, how I had spoken to several people who knew Veronica, or Bessie Moore as she had then been known, how the affair with the young Jack Wimble had led to an unwanted pregnancy and the birth of the girl who would go on to eventually murder her. All of it.

His questions came from different angles as he tried to coax inconsistencies from us, but honesty gives you the benefit of not having to get your stories straight. We answered his questions, rationalised motives and highlighted his own CID's reluctance to investigate further. I wasn't sure that was the most sensible approach, since we could have faced quite some charge sheet if he wished to pursue it. But he did grudgingly acknowledge his department's failings.

He was able to provide us with some good news, and we were relieved to learn that Jack Wimble was out of danger and should, in time, make a full recovery. The same, regrettably, could not be said of the unfortunate Reverend Cackett, who was besieged by demons and would quite possibly never recover completely. Henbane, mandrake and jimsonweed were a vicious cocktail, and only an expert would understand their psychotropic properties fully – an expert such as an advanced botany student. A student like Marianne Brown.

She had grown up detesting everything about her mother, her hatred growing and feeding upon itself. She had kept it well hidden all those years, but now, according to the inspector, she was openly and happily confessing all. She had indeed seduced Tony Dugdale, who had genuinely thought she loved him, and he would have done anything for her, including murder. He was blinded by his misguided love for an unscrupulous and psychologically disturbed woman, a woman who exploited his weaknesses without a hint of remorse.

Eventually, once the inspector was completely satisfied that our intentions were (mostly) honourable, we were released. Not that we had been under arrest, but were "helping the police with their enquiries". I had no doubt that we would be speaking to the inspector again before the case came to trial.

Once again free women, we stepped out into the evening sunshine and breathed the sweet air of freedom. The interview room was bad enough, and we were extremely glad not to be spending a night in the cells at Her Majesty's pleasure. Apparently, Her Majesty had more pressing things to occupy her royal mind this blowy June evening.

The small town of Swanhurst was festooned with

jubilee bunting and balloons strung from windows. Occasionally one of these would pop and scare the life out of passers-by.

'So, what now?' I asked Debbie as we stood on the pavement outside the station house on Gallows Walk. Somewhere not too far away, we could hear cheering and laughing and the sounds of glasses chinking together.

'You mean this minute, or life in general?'

'I was thinking right now, but life in general could also work.'

'Honestly?' she asked. 'Alcohol, and plenty of it.'

I smiled. She was still the same old Debbie. She was taking a knock, to be sure. In fact, her world had just been upended and tossed mercilessly onto the floor, the disparate elements of her existence scattered almost beyond her reach. Almost, but not quite. She was still strong. She still had her boys, she had her home, and she had the chance of a fresh start with everything that she needed.

'Sounds good to me,' I said. 'Let's get drunk in a pub and get chatted up by a couple of hunky farmers. We're both single now.'

At that moment, the door to the police station opened and a tall, handsome and strikingly ginger policeman stepped out.

'Are you ladies okay?' Colin asked.

'Oh we're fine,' I said hastily, realising that he'd probably heard what had just come blurting out of my mouth.

'Only, my shift ends in forty-five minutes, and I wondered if you'd like to meet me for a drink?'

'Both of us?' I asked clumsily.

'Of course. I need to make sure you both keep out of trouble.'

'Sounds good to me,' Debbie said, and I was glad she didn't try to do anything foolish like send me off on a date with the constable, while she went home alone to brood.

'And me,' I agreed. 'Shall we make it The Blue Bell in Downscliffe? Not too far to stagger home from there.'

'Deal,' Colin said. 'I'll meet you in the beer garden around eight-thirty.'

He disappeared back inside the station and Debbie and I strolled arm in arm along to the car park.

'So much for the hunky farmers,' she said with a wink.'

'Never mind. I'm sure there'll be other hunky farmers, or maybe Colin has a hunky policeman pal he could pair you off with?'

'Not a chance!' she exclaimed. 'I'm planning on being youngish, free-ish and single-ish for the time being. Besides, who'd want to shack up with the wife of a murderer?'

'Millions of loons out there. Possibly billions. But you're dead right, quine. Time to live a little again.'

The car park was three quarters empty when we got back to Debbie's Hillman Avenger. Ernie was still parked outside the church, just as Veronica's car had been after she was murdered.

Before getting in, Debbie stopped me. 'To tell you the truth, I'm a bit nervous. I'm on my own and I haven't been in a long time. A long, long time. And I didn't have two ten-year-old boys to look after then. I'm not sure what to do.'

'It's okay. It'll *be* okay. You're not alone. For starters, you're staying at my place tonight and we can drink and talk into the small hours. Your mum can bring the boys over tomorrow and we can explain everything to them then. There's no rush to tell them now.'

'No, I guess you're right.'

'Whatever happens, I'll be right behind you. Okay? We'll have a couple of drinks with the good constable, then the rest of the night is ours.'

She smiled at me, and I could see a genuine warmth in that smile that was rare from her. It would be a long road back, but my friend Debbie would make it, I was sure. She was strong, stronger than she realised, and certainly stronger than me. Eventually I would be able to tell her about Aberdeen, about why I left, about what happened to Fergus's father, and why I couldn't go back.

But that was a story for another day.

Printed in Great Britain
by Amazon